Sherlock Holmes
and
The Tandridge Hall Murder

and other stories

Sherlock Holmes
and
The Tandridge Hall Murder

and other stories

Eddie Maguire

**BREESE
BOOKS
LONDON**

First published in 2000 by
Breese Books Ltd
164 Kensington Park Road, London W11 2ER, England

ISBN: 0 947533 192

Front cover photograph
is reproduced by kind permission of
Brian Girling

Typeset in 11½/14pt Caslon by
Ann Buchan (Typesetters), Middlesex
Printed in the USA

Contents

To my mother Sybil,
always in my memory

Sherlock Holmes and the Tandridge Hall Murder

It was a fine Monday evening in May 1888. As I had not seen Sherlock Holmes for some days, I decided to walk around to Baker Street to the lodgings we had shared before my marriage and spend a little time in his company. I was just turning the corner from Paddington Street, when I almost bumped into the man himself.

'Holmes.'

'My dear Watson. What a pleasant surprise.'

'You are on your way to a case?'

A brief smile flickered across his face. 'Unfortunately no, Doctor. I am merely taking a little exercise for its own sake.'

'Then I will walk with you.'

'Capital. We shall stroll across to Green Park.'

'Green Park,' I said. 'It always seems such a melancholy place.'

'That, Watson, is the precise reason for its attraction to me.'

I laughed. 'You are a strange fellow, Holmes.'

Green Park, despite my foreboding, proved to be quite busy. A large number of gaily-dressed people were taking the air. Holmes and I annexed a park bench nearby to the bandstand.

'You have no case at the moment?' I said.

'Nothing of interest,' said he. 'I realize I have said it before, Watson, but the London criminal is a dull fellow.'

'That is entirely due to your efforts, Holmes. All the most dangerous men are now behind bars.'

'Then I must be thankful for small mercies. But time hangs heavily, Doctor, when the demon of indolence sits upon my shoulder.'

'So, then. We are well met this evening. For I see your mind.'

'Indeed, Watson,' he said, quietly. 'As you have often pointed out, the needle is no friend.'

Feeling it was my duty to keep my companion's attention arrested and his mind occupied, I turned the conversation to his remarkable powers of observation.

'Holmes, you often mention that you are able to observe more than most men. Can you tell me, therefore, what constituted my day's activities?'

Holmes smiled weakly. 'I had done as much within moments of our reunion.'

'And what are your conclusions?'

He gave a sigh. 'Apart from the obvious fact that your wife is presently away from home. That your medical activities have brought you into contact with a lady who is the owner of a black and white dog, which is, I should say, somewhere in size between a terrier and a dalmatian. That tonight you dined on a kipper. And you have given the maid the afternoon off, I can tell you very little.'

'Wonderful,' I laughed. 'But how can you make these assertions? Have you been following me, Holmes?'

'Indeed I have not. The signs are abundantly clear,' said Holmes. 'I warn you, however, when I have explained, you will tell me it was all absurdly simple.'

'My dear fellow, I would never do such a thing. Now tell me about these signs.'

Holmes sat forward on the bench. 'Let us begin with your attire, Doctor. There is dust on your hat and boots, neither of which, I perceive, would long remain in such a state if Mrs Watson was at home. It also implies that the maid is not in residence because she would at least have brushed your hat before letting you loose on London.

'As for the lady with the dog, there are a number of black and white hairs adhering to your trouser legs below the knees. There is also a fresh small tear in your left trouser cuff which is too large to be the work of a terrier, yet too small to be that of a dalmatian.'

'Of course you are correct, Holmes. I thought I had brushed off all the hairs. The lady was Mrs Harrington; you may recall that you assisted her over the loss of a ring some years back. But how could you tell that my client was a lady, not a man?'

'Elementary. Any man who is sufficiently ill to be administered to in his own home would be very unlikely to desire the company of a small animal about his feet. A woman, however, would find great comfort in such a companion.'

'Excellent,' I said. 'But what about the kipper?'

'Ah, the kipper. As you are aware, Doctor, fish has a particularly odorous quality. The kipper produces its own peculiar variety, which can for some time be scented on the breath.'

I laughed. 'You have explained it all. How . . .'

'. . . Absurdly simple?' said Holmes, mildly.

'Touché.'

Our conversation was suddenly interrupted by the arrival

of a very agitated young man, who had come across the park from the direction of the Mall.

'Mr Sherlock Holmes?'

Holmes stood up. 'I am he. But you have the advantage of me.'

'Forgive me, Mr Holmes,' said the young man quickly. 'My name is Harold Norman. I work as a minor official at Lancaster House. This morning, as part of my official duties, I had occasion to speak to your brother, Mr Mycroft Holmes.'

'Brother Mycroft,' muttered Holmes.

'Taking my courage in both hands, I laid before him my problem. Mr Holmes at once advised me to seek you out. I had intended to walk around to your rooms tonight, but then, when I espied you across the park, it occurred to me I might speak to you now. You see, Mr Holmes, I have been the unfortunate witness to a horrible and grisly murder.'

'Good heavens,' I cried. 'If that is so, it is the police you should be informing, not Mr Holmes.'

'If you please, Watson,' said Holmes severely. 'I perceive, Mr Norman, it is because you have spoken to the police that you seek my advice.'

'Indeed, sir,' replied the young man. 'I told the police at once, but they did not believe me.'

'Very well, Mr Norman. If you would be kind enough to step across to my consulting rooms, I shall fortify you with a brandy and soda, then you will tell me the whole story.'

A little later, we were seated in our chairs at 221B Baker Street. Harold Norman was placed on the sofa, drink in hand. Opposite him sat Sherlock Holmes, leaning languidly back in his chair, eyes closed, fingertips together, almost it seemed, in an act of supplication.

'Now, sir. If you would like to begin.'

Norman looked briefly at me. He seemed to be trying to marshal his thoughts. 'Well, Mr Holmes. As you already know, my name is Harold Norman and I work as a minor official at Lancaster House. I am twenty years of age, unmarried and presently live with my uncle at Church End, near Hendon. It is, incidentally, the last stop on the Metropolitan line. There were plans, I believe, to extend the line to the Midlands, but the money ran out.'

Sherlock Holmes opened his eyes. 'The facts, please, Mr Norman, the facts,' he said severely.

'Forgive me, Mr Holmes,' murmured the young man. 'But I confess that I hardly know where to begin.'

'Courage, Mr Norman,' I said. 'Murder is a nasty business and it can shake the hardiest of men.'

Holmes shot me a glance. 'Thank you, Doctor. My apologies, Mr Norman. Please continue.'

'As I was saying, Mr Holmes, I live at Church End. It is quite a rural area. At weekends I have often enjoyed bicycling around the lanes. Indeed, I recently became a member of the Hendon Wheelers Bicycle Club. For weeks now, I have spent my Sundays riding with the club around the towns and villages to the north of Hendon.

'Three weeks ago we rode to Potter's Bar. Last Sunday it was St Albans and yesterday we took a spin out past Hatfield. It was on the way back I sustained a puncture and had to let the rest of the club go on, whilst I mended it. Fortunately we had just passed a big house set in its own grounds. I thought perhaps I might obtain some water there.'

Holmes looked puzzled. 'Why should you need water, Mr Norman?'

'It is the only infallible method of discovering the whereabouts of the hole in the inner tube. You place the tube under water, squeeze it and when the air bubbles appear, there is your hole.'

'Ah,' responded Holmes. 'Thank you. Pray continue.'

'I pushed my bicycle up to the house. I knocked at the front door, but there was no reply. It was then, whilst pondering my next move, that I espied a small dark copse with a sluggish river running through it.'

'You retired there to mend your puncture?' I asked.

'Yes, Dr Watson. It was there that the horrible events I am about to relate took place.'

Holmes sat forward in the chair. 'Now, Mr Norman, you must be quite precise about the events which followed.'

The young man took a sip at his brandy. 'It is an incident that will forever be etched on my mind.'

'Just so,' I asserted. 'But it is vital that you are exact about the circumstances.'

Harold Norman took a deep breath. 'I had just effected a repair and was about to ride away. Then I saw a man approaching. As I felt under some obligation, I decided to wait and explain myself. The man, however, did not appear to have seen me. He was reading something on a piece of paper he was carrying. I was about to call out to him, when I saw another man appear from out of the shadows.

'He was a burly man. I thought at first he was intending to speak with him. But no. He raised his stick and without a word, struck him down.'

'Good heavens!' I cried.

'Quite unnerved by such a vicious and unprovoked attack,

I jumped upon my machine and rode away from the scene. I made immediately for the nearest village to inform the police. Less than ten minutes later I found myself in Mill Street. The constable was having his tea and it took some time to convince him that he should return with me to the house, which I discovered from the constable was called Tandridge Hall. The owner was Sir George Simon.

'This time there was somebody at home. The door was opened by Sir George himself. He was very hot and bothered by my story. He kept on saying it was nonsense, all nonsense.'

'I imagine you insisted on taking Sir George and the constable to the scene of the crime?' said Holmes.

'Yes. But only after much deliberation,' replied Norman. 'It was quite clear to me that neither of them believed a word of my story.'

Holmes took a cigarette from the barrel and offered it to Norman. The young man nodded his approval and lit the cigarette with a spill.

'I perceive that we are now coming to the nub of your narrative,' I remarked.

'Indeed. After much discussion I persuaded them to follow me to the copse. I was fully expecting to show them a mutilated body. Imagine my surprise and consternation when there was nothing to be seen. There was no trace of any crime, nothing.'

'Most interesting,' observed Holmes as he keenly surveyed Norman's face. 'I suppose you were speedily shown the egress?'

The young man smiled grimly. 'At top speed, Mr Holmes. Sir George told me I was either mad or bad and if I did not immediately vacate his land, he would have me put in charge.

'The constable told me I was a fool. He said I was lucky he had better things to do than lock me up, and I should be on my way.

'So you see, Mr Holmes, it was fortunate that I spoke to your brother about the matter. Without his advice I would still be wondering what to do next!'

'Did you consider informing Scotland Yard today?' I said.

'Frankly, no, Dr Watson. For as far as I am concerned, Scotland Yard would no more be likely to believe my story than Sir George or the constable.'

'Quite so, Mr Norman,' retorted Sherlock Holmes. 'My own personal experiences of the Metropolitan policeman show him to have scarcely more imagination than his country compatriot. It is, however, fortunate that I have enough for them all.'

Holmes reached for his pipe. 'Now, Mr Norman, can you describe the two men involved in the murder incident?'

Norman looked a little wryly at Holmes. 'The man who was murdered was perhaps thirty, he was about six feet tall and had quite long black hair. Of his assailant, I am sorry to say I can tell you little. He was always in the shadows. I can only say he was not so tall as his victim, but was considerably more powerfully built.'

'You are sure it was murder?'

'If you had seen the blows that rained down on that poor fellow's head, you would not doubt it.'

'Very well,' said Holmes, decisively. 'If you can tell us no more, then so be it. Now, Mr Norman, will you take Dr Watson and myself to the scene of the crime?'

Norman sprang to his feet. 'Never,' he cried, his voice becoming almost hysterical. 'Nothing would induce me to return to that dreadful spot!'

Holmes laid his hand on the young man's arm. 'I fully understand your reluctance, but you must steel yourself to the inevitable. A terrible crime has been committed. You must show us.'

'Very well, Mr Holmes,' he declared. 'I will come with you, but I will not go to that horrible spot again.'

'Excellent! Now, Mr Norman,' said Holmes, as he quickly thumbed through the Bradshaw, 'if you would be good enough to meet us at King's Cross tomorrow morning, we shall take the ten-fifteen train to Mill Street.'

The next morning Holmes was up bright and early. The prospect of an absorbing case was enough to transform him. At my friend's request, I had stayed the night in my old room. I was gladdened to witness the change. As I sat down to breakfast, Holmes was pacing the room reading from a thick volume.

'Ah, Watson. A capital morning, is it not?'

'Indeed it is, Holmes. But what are you reading there?'

'I am reading up on Sir George Simon. Ah . . . he is the third of his line. Hm . . . Charterhouse, Eton and the Guards; Third Coldstream. He owns land in Lincolnshire and Hertfordshire. Country seat, Tandridge Hall . . . He is the Member of Parliament for the Hertfordshire South Constituency. Sits as a Unionist. His sporting activities include polo, for which he has gained international honours, hunting and rough shooting.

'Ah, now. This is interesting, Watson. Sir George has several black marks against his character. He has twice faced a court accused of common assault.'

'Sir George sounds like a tough customer,' I muttered, buttering my toast. 'But is this interest in the old chap totally warranted?'

Holmes was, as usual, enigmatic in his reply. 'Perhaps, Doctor, then perhaps not.'

He snapped the book shut. 'At any rate, Watson, it is time we were away. I will go downstairs and hail a cab.'

We were met at King's Cross by young Norman. He still seemed to be greatly affected by his ghastly experience. Consequently he proved to be a poor travelling companion. Sherlock Holmes, by comparison, was in the sunniest mood I can remember.

'You have chased your spectre away, Holmes?'

Holmes laughed. 'Not chased away, Doctor; perhaps a temporary banishment.'

A short time later we pulled into Mill Street. It was a quiet country station which had a dozen or so houses marshalled like a battalion around their commander. We engaged a trap from the local public house, the Bull Inn, and were soon rattling along a leafy country lane.

Suddenly Norman broke his silence. 'There, Mr Holmes. The gates of Tandridge Hall.'

Holmes reined in the horse. 'Perhaps in the circumstances, discretion should be the better part of valour. We should not enter boldly, but with caution. If you wait here with the trap, Watson, Norman and I will go on foot from here.'

Norman, as if galvanized, grabbed the sleeve of my companion. 'No, Mr Holmes,' he declared. 'I cannot go back there.'

Holmes gave an almost inaudible sigh. 'Very well, Mr Norman, but you must at least direct me to the scene of the crime.'

Sherlock Holmes, however, was not absent for long. For no sooner had he slipped through the gates, he was accosted by two large men who demanded to know his business.

At the same moment a large bearded man in his fifties rode up on a white cob. 'Who the devil are you and what are you doing on my land?'

'Sir George Simon, I believe,' said Holmes coolly. 'My name is Sherlock Holmes. Across the road is my friend, Dr Watson. With him is Harold Norman, whom I believe you already know.'

The baronet glowered. 'Holmes,' he growled. 'Yes, I have heard of you. An infernal busybody.'

Holmes smiled and bowed low. 'You are too kind, sir.'

'Well, what the blazes do you want?'

'It is my understanding that on Sunday last a cold-blooded murder took place in these grounds. I am here to investigate.'

Sir George surveyed Holmes with a contemptuous glare and pointed his riding whip in Norman's direction.

'You have been listening to the fantasies of that young donkey?' he cried.

'I believe him to be telling the truth.'

'Then you are a fool.'

Sherlock Holmes bowed once more. 'Thank you again.'

At this Sir George seemed to lose all self-control. 'Get off my land,' he screamed. 'Jenkins, Alexander, eject this man forcibly. Do not allow him or his rabble back through this gate!'

He reined his cob around and spurred it away. Moments later Holmes was spun roughly into the dusty lane by Sir George's men.

'Holmes!' I cried, helping him to his feet. 'Are you hurt?'

Sherlock Holmes gave a light laugh as he dusted himself

down. 'No, my dear Watson. I am not hurt. I am, however, determined to return and examine Sir George's land, with or without his approbation.'

'Indeed?' I said. 'How so?'

'That would be telling, Doctor, but for the present, let us return to the Bull Inn at Mill Street, where we may lay our plans.'

Upon our return, Holmes secured a private sitting room and the promise of an excellent lunch. Young Norman sat in the window seat watching some of the locals engaging in a darts match.

Holmes pulled me to one side. 'Now, Watson. If you would be good enough to obtain exact directions to the scene of the crime from our young friend, I will endeavour to find out a little of the local gossip about the denizens of Tandridge Hall.'

After lunch, Norman and I took our drinks onto the front step of the inn. A few minutes later we were joined by a rustic gentleman.

'Mornin', gents. A fine day for the farmer.'

'Indeed, it is, sir,' I agreed. 'Are you a local, or are you passing through?'

'No, sir. I'm just an itinerant worker seeking to earn a crust. I was thinking of asking up at the big house back along.'

'Tandridge Hall.'

'Ar. That be the one.'

'My dear man, I would advise you to avoid that place like the plague.'

'That is a pity, Watson, for it is vital that I get temporary employment there.'

'Holmes!'

'The same.'

'You are going back to the Hall?'

'Indeed. I must return. No, do not concern yourself. If you, who know me well, cannot recognize me, it is unlikely that Sir George will.'

'Very well. Here is your map. I have written full instructions. Good luck, Holmes.'

Harold Norman gave a wan smile, 'Yes, Mr Holmes. Good luck!'

It was past six pm when Holmes returned. Of his adventures he would say nothing. 'A wash and a meal first, Doctor. Then we can talk.'

Very soon, however, Holmes was comfortably ensconced by a crackling fire, puffing away appreciatively at his pipe, a brandy and soda by his elbow.

Young Norman, who had fidgeted throughout, could restrain his impatience no longer and blurted out: 'For heaven's sake, Mr Holmes, will you tell me if you were able to uncover the truth?'

'Oh,' said Holmes, casually. 'There was undoubtedly a murder done at Tandridge Hall.'

'Look out, Holmes. I think our friend is fainting.'

Norman had slipped almost out of his chair.

'Here, my boy,' said Holmes, forcing a little of the brandy and soda between his lips. 'Drink this!'

With a great effort Norman regained his composure. 'You must forgive me, gentlemen. Until now, I was almost convinced that I had imagined the whole event.'

'Now, tell me, Holmes. How did you discover the truth?'

'You will, of course, recollect this noontide I made my way in disguise in order to obtain employment. When I arrived at the gate, Sir George's two men were still in attendance. There was a third man present. He turned out to be Jonas Baker, the estate manager.

' "What do you want here?" he demanded.

' "If you please, sir," I said. "I am looking for an afternoon's employment. I am a bodger by trade, but if you have any wood cuttings or kindling, I'm your man."

'He looked me up and down for a few moments, then he asked me my name and where I was from. I told him my name was Mycroft and I was from Lincolnshire. He seemed pleased to hear the name of my adopted county. "Lincolnshire, eh!" he said. "Sir George's ancestral home. Very well, Mycroft, come with me." '

Holmes chuckled softly. 'Taking up my borrowed bags of tools, I followed him. I was delighted to discover that he was taking me to the little copse so excellently described by Norman. He pointed out a stack of logs and beside it two barrels. "Here, I want these barrels filled with kindling by tonight."

' "How much will you pay me?" I asked, playing up my part for all it was worth.

' "You will receive two shillings and if your work is adequate, you will be given an evening meal with the other servants."

'I set to work right away. After a few moments Mr Baker seemed satisfied and walked away in the direction of the Hall.

'The very moment he was out of sight I began a close investigation of my surroundings. I could see at once, Mr Norman, that there still remained traces of two men. The first, I deduced was walking slowly. The other I perceived had been waiting for some time because the grass beneath one of the larger trees had been flattened. I also discovered this.' Holmes reached into an inside pocket and produced a cigarette end. 'You will note the red crescent near the end.'

'It may prove to be significant?'

'Yes, Mr Norman. It may.'

Holmes reached out and tapped his pipe on the fire-dog. 'A closer inspection of the area revealed the presence of blood on the grass. I also saw two furrows had been scraped in the soft earth between the trees and the water.'

'As if someone had been dragged along,' cried Norman.

'Exactly. The river bank is soft and boggy. There is a shallow area with many reeds. It was there I discovered a clear footprint. It was a large square-toed boot, sunken greatly into the soft earth.'

'The mark of a very heavy man,' I said.

'Or of a normal man carrying a body.'

'Good Lord!'

'I have made a quick sketch of the imprint here.' He handed me a page torn from his notebook. 'You will note the peculiar V-shaped nick in the heel.'

'Well done, Mr Holmes.'

Sherlock Holmes scraped out the bowl of his pipe and tapped it once again on the fire-dog. 'As I mentioned, there were many reeds at the water's edge. It was there that I found the prize I had been seeking. I found a small rowing boat hidden almost completely from sight. The boat was covered with a tarpaulin. Under the tarpaulin, I discovered the bloody corpse of a young man.'

'Great Scot!'

'You see, Mr Holmes, Dr Watson. It was just as I told you.'

'Indeed, Mr Norman. Now, Doctor, tell me what do you make of this?'

'It is a scrap of paper . . . with something written on it.

Where did you find this, Holmes?'

'It was in the corpse's left hand. It is obviously a fragment torn from a larger sheet. In all probability, the paper he was reading when he was set upon.'

'But what do you make of it, Holmes?'

'It is doubtless a note arranging a meeting.'

At that moment there came a heavy knock at the door.

'Come in, Lestrade,' cried Holmes.

'Lestrade?' I exclaimed.

The door opened and a thin-faced weasly man entered.

'My dear fellow. Come in and warm yourself by the fire.'

'Now then, Mr Holmes,' said Lestrade in his best Scotland Yard manner. 'What is all this about a murder? I was just about to go home for my supper when I received your telegram.'

'Thank you for coming so swiftly, Lestrade. Your promptness does you great credit.'

The detective preened himself. 'Well now, sir. You have been able to help me in some little matters in the past, so I suppose it's only right and proper for me to come to your aid when called.'

'And so you have, my dear Lestrade,' laughed Holmes. 'So you have. No, do not bother to remove your coat. Come, Watson, Mr Norman. We will now pay another visit on Sir George Simon.'

*

It was a little under half an hour later, when Sherlock Holmes, Mr Norman, Inspector Lestrade and myself were face to face with Sir George, who received us in the gun room.

'Now, what the devil is this all about?' he demanded.

'A remarkable display of weapons,' observed Holmes, taking down a small pepperbox.

'Answer me, sir,' cried the baronet.

'I expect you are a good shot,' continued Holmes, mildly.

'This is quite intolerable.'

'How are your reflexes, Sir George,' said Holmes, as he threw the pepperbox at our reluctant host.

'Very good I see,' he said, as Sir George caught the pistol in his left hand.

'You will excuse Mr Holmes,' grunted Lestrade, attempting to assert his authority over the proceedings. 'But there has been a particularly horrible murder here at Tandridge Hall and I am here to investigate it.'

Sir George Simon grew quite pale and spoke in a more measured tone. 'Surely, Inspector, you do not believe this cock-and-bull story?'

'Whether I do or whether I do not believe it, sir, I am obliged to inquire further.' He replaced his hat onto his head. 'Now, Sir George, if you will please accompany me to the scene of the crime, where, before the light fades, I will begin my investigation.'

'Good old Lestrade,' exclaimed Holmes. 'Come, Watson. Let us follow the leader. Mr Norman, you will remain here?'

'Indeed, sir.'

'Very good . . . Oh dear, I appear to have forgotten my pipe. Mr Norman, do you have a cigarette? . . . Ah, thank you. Now lead on, Lestrade. Lead on.'

Lestrade was first to the boat. He pulled back the tarpaulin and exposed a terrible sight. The bloody corpse of a young man lay at the bottom of the boat.

It was Sir George who spoke first.

'Good grief. It is Harris, my head groom.'

My professional instincts quickly came to the fore. 'We should move this poor fellow to a more suitable place as soon as possible.'

'Perhaps the ice house,' said Sir George.

'That is an excellent suggestion. Now, if you would help me, Holmes.'

'Certainly, Doctor.'

After some effort, we wrapped Harris in the tarpaulin and carried him to the beehive-shaped building some yards away, and laid him on a table which might have been constructed for the task.

'Now, Watson, a quick examination.' Holmes took a piece of rag and wiped the face of the corpse. 'Ah . . . what do you make of this, Doctor?'

'The back of his skull is depressed slightly and the carotid artery has been severed. He was clearly bludgeoned unconscious, then his throat was cut. He undoubtedly bled to death.'

There was an exclamation of horror from Sir George. Sherlock Holmes gave a grim smile. 'Which explains the considerable amount of blood on the grass.'

'Indeed.'

'Can you say if the slash of the knife came from the left or the right?'

'Undoubtedly the right. It was done by a left-handed man. Or at any rate, a man using his left hand. Look, the cut is much deeper here on the right where the cut begins. Here on the left where it ends, the cut is more shallow.'

'So where does that lead us, Mr Holmes?' said Lestrade.
'To a tall, well-built man who is left-handed, who smokes Turkish cigarettes and is without scruples.'

Lestrade grunted. 'I think it is pretty clear, Mr Holmes, who the guilty party is. I have no doubt it is clear to you also?'

'Indeed, Lestrade. You are correct. I know who our murderer is. But humour me a while longer before you do your duty.'

Lestrade's face bore an expression which resembled that of a dog deprived of its bone. 'Very well, Mr Holmes. I will not rob you of your fun.'

On our journey back to the Hall, my eyes fell upon our host. He was white-faced and silent, his bluster and aggression quelled by recent events. Sherlock Holmes broke into his reverie. 'Um, Sir George, do you have a cigarette? My pipe, you know.'

The baronet grumbled to himself but nevertheless produced his case from which Holmes helped himself.

'Thank you, Sir George.'

Back in the room we discovered Norman nervously pacing up and down.

'Well, Mr Holmes?' he cried as we entered.

'Everything is in order, Mr Norman. We have our man.'

'You have? That is good news. But what of the motive?'

'The motive was revenge, Mr Norman, simple revenge.'

We were interrupted by a knock at the door. It was one of the Hall's army of servants. In his hand he held a telegram addressed to Sherlock Holmes. Holmes opened the envelope and quickly scanned the contents. 'Excellent,' he said, 'Excellent.'

'Now, Mr Holmes,' said Lestrade, 'if you will now let me do my duty. . .?'

'Of course, Lestrade.' Holmes held out his hand. 'If you will give me your handcuffs, I will slip them on to the culprit for you.'

'Thank you, Mr Holmes. Here.'

There was a clinking of chains, a snapping of springs and a violent start from the prisoner.

'Now, Mr Harold Norman, I have you.'

'Mr Holmes,' cried Lestrade.

'Holmes?' I ejaculated.

'What the devil does this mean?' exclaimed Sir George.

It was during this moment of hiatus, that Norman made a dash for the window. But Holmes was upon him like a tiger.

There was a heavy crash as both men hit the floor. One smashing blow from the right hand of Sherlock Holmes was sufficient to knock the fight out of Norman. Holmes dragged his man to his feet and threw him into an armchair.

'Now, Mr Holmes,' said Lestrade, 'will you tell me what this is about?'

'Yes, Holmes,' I rejoined. 'How can the murderer be Norman? I was under the impression that it was Sir George.'

Sir George Simon sat heavily into another armchair with a look of total bemusement on his face.

'Mr Holmes, I am simply unable to comprehend what is happening.'

'To begin with, Sir George,' said Holmes, 'Norman has a confession to make.' He turned and glared at his prisoner. 'Do you not?'

'Curse you. Yes, it was I. But how you discovered the truth is beyond me. You are a magician.'

Holmes laughed. 'Not a magician, Mr Norman. Merely a humble seeker of the truth.'

'But, Mr Holmes, what is the truth?' demanded Lestrade.

Sherlock Holmes, keen as ever to enjoy the theatricality of the moment, addressed Norman. 'It was a good plan, was it not? It was in order to right an old wrong?'

Norman nodded. 'It was on Sunday morning, Sir George, that Norman arrived at your gates. Hiding his bicycle in a convenient hedge, he made his way to the stable block . . . You will stop me when I go wrong, Mr Norman . . . There on a convenient table, he left a note which read something like — "Harris, come at once to the copse by the river. Do not delay. Urgent. George Simon." '

Norman grunted his assent.

'Such an unexpected appeal would result in Harris following instructions without delay or question. Norman was waiting in the copse. For how long did you wait?'

'I was forced to wait for about ten minutes.'

'Indeed. Long enough to smoke one cigarette.'

Holmes produced a butt and held it up for our inspection. 'When Harris arrived, you stepped out from behind a tree and struck him down using a handy chunk of wood taken from the pile by the copse. Then you proceeded to slash his throat with a knife you obtained from the stable yard.' Holmes reached again into his pocket and threw the bloody instrument onto the table.

'It was under the corpse in the boat. I discovered it when you removed the body, Watson.'

Holmes turned again to Norman. 'You waited for the blood to stop, then you dragged the dead man to the boat and covered him with a tarpaulin.'

'The note, Holmes?' I asked. 'What of the note?'

'Ah yes. The note. It was a clever artifice, Mr Norman. You yourself tore the corner off and forced it into the corpse's hand.'

'Indeed?' I exclaimed. 'But why?'

'Presently, Doctor. Mr Norman, you then returned to the road, collected your bicycle and rode off to Mill Street to your interview with the local constable. When you returned to the Hall, you showed a different part of the copse to Sir George and the constable, thereby convincing them that it was all nonsense.

'The very next morning you were fortunate enough to encounter my brother, Mycroft. I do not know if it was a lucky coincidence, but it was a useful encounter in all events and it established your bonafides.

'You next waited at your window until you espied Dr Watson and myself in Green Park. It was then that you set into action the chain of events we have just experienced.

'You had carefully laid a trail of clues, which you know I could hardly fail to observe. This cigarette end, identical to the brand smoked by Sir George. The mark of a large riding boot. And a description of a heavy-set man seen attacking Harris.

'It was your intent to establish Sir George as the prime suspect. You relied on the planted evidence and Sir George's reputation for hot-headed outbursts. You saw your opportunity and you took it.'

'Damn you!' cried Norman.

'Thank you,' said Holmes, lightly.

'What of the note?' I said again.

'There is no doubt that a minute inspection of this room will uncover the note, and a further inspection of the stables, a pair of square-toed boots. Norman has had plenty of opportunity to secrete them somewhere.'

'That is why he would not come with us just now?'

'Exactly,' Holmes smiled briefly. 'Such evidence would prove to be damning. Lestrade was already convinced of Sir George's guilt. Were you not, Lestrade?'

Lestrade gave a cough.

'Further evidence supplied by yourself, Watson, would have convinced any jury in England. The slash to the corpse's throat ran right to left and Sir George is . . .'

'Left-handed,' I cried.

'Just so. It was a perfect case.'

'But, good heavens, man, what was his motive?' exclaimed the baronet.

'Motive. I'll give you motive, damn you!' cried the prisoner, scrambling to his feet. 'You, Sir high and mighty George Simon. You with your money and your position. What do you care for others? What have you ever cared for the poor man? The worker you so casually discharge? What do you care for his wife, his children? They are all as nothing to you.

'You ask about a motive, Sir George. I'll give you a motive. Four years ago you were running a polo team. Do you remember your head groom, Jim Norman? Do you also remember how Jim Norman begged you not to sack him after your ponies became ill? Do you recall how he cried at your feet for mercy? And do you also remember how you had him thrown off your land without a penny piece in compensation?'

'Oh,' muttered Sir George, 'Yes, I remember him. A pony purchased by him passed a sickness onto the whole stables.'

'He did no such thing. It was all the fault of Harris. The man you promoted to head groom. The man who covered up his own guilt and let an innocent man be discharged.'

'But I do not understand,' said Sir George. 'What is it to you?'

'It may please you to know, Sir George, that Jim Norman was my father.'

'Your father,' muttered Sir George Simon.

'It may also please you to know that after my father was discharged, he could find no work. Your blacklisting of him meant he was unemployable. Very soon we were paupers, living off the local parish. A year later the whole family was admitted into the Handwell Workhouse. The family was split up. My father and myself in one hall, my mother and sisters in the other.

'It was after six months of enduring this daily ignominy that my parents died of influenza, and my sisters were put into service. A few weeks later a kindly uncle came into a few pounds and was able to assist me. He took me into his home and found a minor post in the Civil Service.

'That was two and a half years ago. Two and a half years in which I have schemed and plotted my revenge. I have done for Harris. And now, Sir George, I'll do for you!'

Norman's last words rose to a shout as he threw himself at the baronet. But if Norman was quick to move, Holmes was quicker. This time a left fist crashed into the face of the young man, who fell senseless to the floor.

'Well, Lestrade,' observed Holmes. 'I believe we have heard enough.'

'Indeed we have, Mr Holmes,' agreed the inspector. 'I must say it was a very neat piece of work.'

Holmes smiled. 'Elementary, Lestrade. Elementary.'

The train puffed slowly through the Hertfordshire countryside. Holmes seemed to have sprawled along almost the whole carriage.

'Well, my dear fellow,' I said, 'You look quite relaxed.'

'Um. It was a satisfactory case. Most stimulating.'

'It was certainly a tragic case.'

'Indeed.'

'Tell me, Holmes. When did you first suspect that things were not quite what they seemed to be?'

Holmes smiled and adopted a more conventional sitting position. 'It was when I discovered the lack of footprints.'

'What on earth do you mean?'

'You will, no doubt, remember that Norman claimed to have observed two men in the copse?'

'I do.'

'Then you will agree, Watson, it follows that there should have been present three sets of footprints. One set for each of the persons involved.'

'Undoubtedly so, but . . .'

'There were, however, but two sets of footprints. One set for the attacker and one set for his victim. But of the observer there was no trace. As you will remember, Watson, I have often complained about too many footprints, but never in my career have I encountered too few.'

'Well, well,' I mused, 'Norman left you a trail of clues to follow, but for all his cleverness, he forgot the third set of footprints.'

'Exactly.'

'You explain it all, Holmes, except . . .'

'Except?'

'The telegram you received at Tandridge Hall. Who sent it?'

'It was from my brother, Mycroft. When I sent for Lestrade, I also contacted Mycroft. I laid before him the bare facts. I asked about Norman's bonafides and told him of my suspicions.' Holmes reached for his coat pocket and handed the telegram to me. It read:

NORMAN UNDOUBTEDLY GUILTY.

ADVISE IMMEDIATE ARREST.

MYCROFT

Holmes smiled. 'My brother is the soul of brevity.'

'So I see.'

'You will understand, Watson, when a mind with a capacity so much greater than my own comes to the same conclusion, there can be no doubt that it is the correct conclusion.'

'The two greatest minds in Europe in collaboration.'

'Why, thank you, Doctor,' said Holmes, bowing slightly.

There was, however, to be something of a sequel to these events. Some six months had elapsed since our investigation and the matter had completely slipped my mind. Then one day in November, having completed my rounds, I returned to my consulting rooms.

As I warmed myself by the fire, I took the opportunity to glance through my copy of the *Daily Telegraph*. It was when I turned to the political page that I was reminded of our adventures at Tandridge Hall. The headline ran:

SIR GEORGE SIMON, CHAMPION OF THE POOR,

CALLS FOR AN END TO THE WORKHOUSE

AND THE POOR LAW ACT

It was later the same afternoon when I called on Sherlock Holmes. As I entered the sitting room I espied a full pipe and a brandy and soda on the table by my old armchair.

'Holmes. You are expecting me?'

'You have read your *Telegraph*, Watson?'

'Indeed, but . . .'

'Then you could hardly have failed to see the article about Sir George Simon. You had to come to tell me.'

I sighed. 'Of course, you are right, Holmes. You read me like a book. But the news. What do you make of it?'

'It is evident that, like St Paul, Sir George has seen the error of his ways. Only his particular road to Damascus took him via the workhouse and the graveyard. He has learnt a salutary lesson, Watson, and that is, most of the poor are not poor by chance and too many find themselves thus through the high-handed action of others.'

'Then let us sincerely hope that Sir George may convince others in a position of power and influence that it is so.'

'However,' said Holmes, brightening up, 'It is a splendid day. What would you say to another turn in Green Park?'

'An excellent suggestion, Holmes. But there is one activity from which I strongly recommend you to desist.'

'Yes, my dear Watson?'

'It is the one where you talk to strangers. It seems to get you into too much trouble!'

A Death at the Cricket

(Being a reprint of the original 1896 publication,
privately published by John H. Watson, MD)

I t was the high summer of 1896. Sherlock Holmes and I
had recently brought to a successful conclusion the affair
of the beryl coronet. Holmes, however, was far from the
picture of contentment one might have supposed him to
be after such a brilliant coup. He was tetchy and edgy. It
was a symptom I well knew and clearly recognized. His
spirit so recently at its zenith had quickly slipped to its
nadir.

We had settled down to breakfast which I attacked with
my usual relish. Holmes, however, merely toyed with his
egg.

'Come along, old fellow. You really must cheer up. This
moping about is doing you no good,' I said.

Holmes cast a jaundiced eye in my direction. 'You mean
it is doing you no good, Doctor,' he retorted.

'Then perhaps it is doing neither of us any good,' I
replied soothingly.

'But there is nothing to relieve me from the mundane.
Nothing of interest, Watson.' He took a sheaf of papers
from his inside pocket and threw them on the table. 'These
are the cases I have recently worked upon. Read the contents.

You will quickly observe them to be more banality and triviality.'

I was about to argue the point with him, when Mrs Hudson arrived to remove the breakfast tray.

'There is a letter for you, Dr Watson,' she said. 'It came a few minutes ago.' She retrieved the tray and looked doubtfully at Holmes who had left most of his breakfast untouched. She made no comment, however, and silently withdrew.

I took the envelope from the table and examined it. 'Why, it is from Foster Stamford. You remember Stamford, Holmes?'

Sherlock Holmes looked up from his notes. 'Should I?' he said tersely.

'You should. He is the fellow who introduced us.' I tore open the envelope and read the contents.

'This is all very interesting, Holmes. Foster is at present managing a medical cricketers' XI. He says they are touring the Home Counties. Next weekend they are to play Lord Sheffield's XI at Sheffield Park and he has invited us to join him there. What do you think of that?'

For the first time in days, Holmes looked interested in a topic.

'Lord Sheffield,' he said. 'Is he not a patron of something or other?'

'My dear fellow,' I said, marvelling at my friend's supreme ignorance, 'he is almost certainly cricket's greatest benefactor. Single-handedly he has promoted the Sussex club to national prominence.'

'He is a rich man, then.'

'But he uses his money wisely, Holmes,' I said, warmly. 'Those who know him rejoice at the sound of his name.'

Holmes stood up and moved across to the bookshelf where he kept his index. He reached out and ran a long tapered finger along the row of volumes until he found the book he was seeking, and took it down.

'Let me see. Hmm . . . Lord Sheffield. Ah, here we are. Henry North Holroyd, third earl of Sheffield of Dunsmore Meath. Baron Sheffield of Roscommon in Ireland and Baron Sheffield of Sheffield, Yorkshire. Country seat, Sheffield Park, Sussex. Born Portland Place 1832, so he is sixty-four. Educated Eton. Diplomatic service, served in Constantinople and Copenhagen. Member of Parliament for East Sussex from 1868 until the death of his father in 1876 when he succeeded to the peerage. Ah now. This will interest you, Watson. He has been a member of the MCC since 1855. As Viscount Pevensey, he opened Sheffield Park in 1866 for the free public attendance at cricket matches arranged by himself. In 1892 he presented to the cricket boards of New South Wales, Victoria and South Australia, a trophy which has become popularly known as the "Sheffield Shield". Hmm . . . It appears he is also unmarried . . . You will also appreciate this, Watson. He is well known in the county of Sussex for his great generosity. Well now, his Lordship appears to be an interesting sort of fellow, Doctor. Perhaps I should meet him.'

Much excited by the prospect of extracting Holmes from his black cloud of depression, I asked him eagerly, 'You will come with me to Sussex?'

'Well now,' said Holmes, thoughtfully. 'Judging by the mundane quality of the cases presently under consideration, making the acquaintance of such an uplifting character as Lord Sheffield can only result in a considerable improvement to my state of mind. Yes, Watson, I shall come to Sussex with you.'

'Excellent,' I cried.

It was a bright and sunny day which found us on our journey to Sussex. Sherlock Holmes had, for once, disavowed himself of his usual attire and was sitting opposite me in the railway carriage, cane in hand, resplendently attired in a boater, a blazer of Prussian blue, and white flannels. As for myself, I was hardly less well turned out, in a cap, which I wore at an appropriately rakish angle, and a matching green blazer with cream flannels.

It was a Bank Holiday weekend and the train was full of holidaymakers. 'Arries and 'Arriettes all bright and gay, laden with their bags and trunks, carrying sandwiches, bottles of sticky lemonade and cold tea, sufficient to sustain them on their sojourn to the seaside.

The train was joined en route by several others who were clearly destined for Sheffield Park. At Croydon, a young, dark-haired man, short and quick moving, got into our carriage. He threw down a long canvas bag with strong leather handles. I recognized him immediately as Robert Abel, the Surrey opening bat.

Mr Abel tipped his hat and sat down next to Holmes. 'Good day, gentlemen.'

'A very good day to you, sir,' I said, eagerly. 'Holmes, this is Mr Bob Abel. You will recall me telling you of the one hundred and forty-four runs he so recently scored against Australia.'

The young man cast a shrewd glance in the direction of my travelling companion. 'Mr Holmes?' he said, 'Surely you are Mr Sherlock Holmes of Baker Street?'

Holmes held out his hand. 'I am he.'

'Then we are well met,' said the sportsman. 'About a year ago you were generous enough to offer your help to my

aunt, Miss Margery Dickson, of Clapham. You were able
to rescue her from the clutches of an evil and rapacious
landlord.'

'Indeed,' said Holmes, darkly. 'He was a thoroughly unpleasant character. It was a task which I must confess to
enjoying, Mr Abel.'

At East Grinstead, the train had just begun puffing its
way out of the station when a huge fair-haired man hur-
dled the little fence which lay alongside the platform, and
ran pell-mell after the train.

Abel stood up and peered out of the carriage window.
'My word. It's old Bonnor.' He opened the door and yelled
out to the young giant, 'Here, old man, jump in here.'

A large canvas bag was thrown onto the carriage floor.
Presently it was joined there by the young man himself
who lay for some moments, gasping for breath.

Abel slammed the carriage door. Then he made the
formal introductions. 'Mr Holmes, Dr Watson. The breathless wreck at your feet is Mr George Bonnor. George, meet
Mr Sherlock Holmes and Dr Watson.'

Bonnor saluted us, scrambled to his feet, then collapsed
into his seat. 'Jeez, Bob,' he gasped, 'I didn't think I would
make it.'

Abel laughed. 'Gentlemen,' he said, 'this is what they
send over to us from Australia. Great weaklings. You would
hardly know it, but this fellow is known as the Australian
Hercules.'

Bonnor snorted, and for a few moments the two cricketers traded insults in a manner in which only the best of
friends can achieve.

Very soon the conversation turned to the cricket. Sherlock
Holmes, who earnestly believed in the maxim that the only

thing worse than taking part in sport was talking about it, made himself comfortable in the corner seat and dozed until our train clanked and clattered into Sheffield Park station.

A trap was waiting for us in the station yard. We piled our bags onto the vehicle and the four of us, all being young active men, decided to walk the mile or so to his Lordship's front door.

'Here we are,' said Abel, as the door was opened by a small dark man of about five and twenty. 'Gentlemen, this image is Harold Price. He earns his living by sucking up to his Lordship.'

Price scowled at the Surrey man. 'Come in, please, gentlemen,' he muttered, ushering us into the hallway. 'Lord Sheffield is receiving visitors in the yellow room. Whom shall I announce?'

Abel laughed. 'I expect the old man knows me well enough by now, but you can tell him, that along with George Bonnor, Australia's premier batsman, the renowned Sherlock Holmes and Dr Watson are gracing him with their presence.'

Price said nothing. He turned on his heel and quickly disappeared into an adjacent room.

A little taken aback by Abel's manner, I said, 'You are always so forthright in your language?'

'With Price,' he said, 'it is the only way. The fellow is a complete bounder. Goodness knows why his Lordship tolerates him.'

'Has Price been in the employ of Lord Sheffield for very long?' said Holmes.

Abel rubbed his chin reflectively. 'He has only worked for his Lordship since March, when Aitchesson, his predecessor, was injured in a riding accident.'

Moments later Price returned an
ence of Lord Sheffield. He greeted
with cordiality, but with Bonnor and
little of the reserve for which the Englis
Indeed, he clasped them warmly by the
them as if they were his own two sons.
lies the innate magic of our great summer
ability to bring together so many otherwise dis

After supper, Sherlock Holmes and Lord
came engrossed in the subject of crime and i
For myself, I sought out the company of Foster

'Hello, old man,' said Stamford, smiling and ou
hand. 'I do not have to ask what you have been ge
to these past few years.'

I smiled in return and shook the proffered hand. '
Stamford. The same thing cannot be said about you
When we last spoke, you were about to become Br
youngest surgeon. Now I find you managing a med.
cricketing tour.'

Stamford sighed. 'I'm afraid a dose of enteric fever two
years ago, when I was in Rhodesia, put paid to any such
notions, Watson. I was left with hands so shaky, I was
unable to continue in my profession.'

— He held up his hands for inspection. The tremor was all
too obvious.

'My dear fellow,' I said, 'I am truly sorry.'

Stamford smiled. 'Not to worry, Watson. I was fortunate
enough to gain help and assistance from an old colleague.
You will remember Sir Angus Wilson?'

'Indeed. He was my senior by two years in medical
school.'

'Well, Sir Angus knew of a fellow who was keen to sell

ractice in nearby Forest Row. He put in a good word
ne. It is not a very absorbing practice, but it keeps me in
ds, so I cannot complain.'

Wonderful,' I said. 'But what of the cricket?'

Last summer, Sir Angus telegraphed me to ask if I could
are the time to organize a match between the hospital
am and one of the local sides. I was able to arrange two
xtures and it was all a great success. This year they have
sked me to run the whole thing. Well, I agreed, and here
we are.'

'Are you quite happy?'

'Indeed. My only concern is that nowadays I am a martyr
to insomnia, which keeps me up and about at all hours.'

It was after midnight when Lord Sheffield bade us
goodnight. Holmes and I had been appointed to adjoining
rooms overlooking the rose garden, the intoxicating perfume
of the flowers filling the air. Notwithstanding, it was a mere
moment before I found myself deep in the arms of Morpheus.

'Watson, Watson, wake up, old man.' It was the voice of
Sherlock Holmes drawing me back into the waking world.
In the half-light, I reached for my watch.

'Holmes, what is the matter? Good heavens, it is hardly
half past five. Has something happened?'

'It has, Doctor. There has been a serious accident. It is
Stamford.'

'Stamford?' I cried, throwing back the bedclothes.

'Yes, please hurry. I will wait for you in his Lordship's
study.'

I hurriedly threw on my clothes and stopping only to
give my hair a perfunctory brush, I rapidly made my way
downstairs.

Lord Sheffield's study was quite full. Holmes and his Lordship stood by the window. Price and Bonnor were conversing by the fire. Arthur Onions and Charles Mortimore, two medical students, were talking to an agitated man I had not seen before. His manner was apologetic, yet defiant at the same time.

'There's no doubt about it, the gentleman stepped straight under my wheels. It was his own fault, begging your pardon,' he said.

'What has happened?' I said. 'Where is Stamford?'

Holmes moved across the room and laid his hand upon my shoulder. For a fleeting moment I saw something in his face that I had never before witnessed. It was a look of tenderness. 'I am sorry, Watson. Stamford is dead. They are just bringing him up to the house.'

'But what has happened?' I asked once more.

'He walked straight under my wheels, sir,' said the agitated man, also repeating himself.

'This gentleman is James Sidgwick,' said Holmes. 'He is a drayman for the Brittles brewery of East Grinstead.' He turned to the drayman. 'Now, Mr Sidgwick, will you please repeat to Dr Watson what you have told me.'

Sidgwick cleared his throat. 'It's like this, sir. I was just driving my dray past the entrance to the house. As I turned at the crossroads, the gentleman seemed to just step out into the road from the verge. He was under my wheels afore I knew it.'

There was a knock at the door. It was Singleton, Lord Sheffield's head groom. He looked flustered. 'We have placed Mr Stamford in the library, sir,' he said. 'But I must tell you, he is very strangely dressed.'

Sherlock Holmes looked up from his reverie. 'What do you mean?' he said, sharply.

'Well, Sir. He was half undressed, if you take my meaning. Sort of dishevelled like.'

Holmes was through the open doorway almost before Singleton had completed his sentence. 'Come, Watson,' he said over his shoulder.

Stamford was laid on the library floor with a white sheet covering him. Holmes pulled back the sheet.

'Well, Doctor. What do you make of that?'

Poor Stamford was indeed dressed in a singular fashion. He wore a dark tweed jacket, beneath which he still had on his nightshirt which had been quickly tucked into light grey flannels.

Holmes pulled back the sheet a little more and revealed Stamford's feet. 'Good heavens. He is wearing only one boot.'

Holmes turned to Singleton. 'Did you observe the other boot?'

'No, sir, I did not.'

'Very well. We must search for it.'

'I will accompany you, Holmes,' I said.

'Thank you, Doctor. Perhaps you will be kind enough to ask Mr Sidgwick to come along as well.'

Moments later, Holmes, followed by myself, Sidgwick, Singleton, Onions and Mortimore, was heading quickly for the road to inspect the place where poor Stamford had met his death.

The road which passed Sheffield Park was both narrow and overhung with trees. It was skirted on one side by the estate wall and by the trees on the other.

We arrived at the spot indicated by Sidgwick. The dray was pulled up onto the neatly cut verge, the horse attended to by a boy, whom Sidgwick introduced as his son.

Sherlock Holmes instructed the assembly in their duties. The students were ordered to keep any traffic from using the road, whilst Holmes carefully scrutinized the area. 'Now, Mr Sidgwick, from where exactly did Mr Stamford appear?'

'He must have bin astanding in the lee of that little gateway, there,' said the drayman. 'Like I said afore, he just seemed to step in my path.'

'Very good,' said Holmes. 'Now, gentlemen. If you will please retire, I shall inspect the road.'

It was scarcely five minutes later when Holmes discovered the missing boot. It was found near to the gateway. Holmes held it up for our benefit. He then began to jump up and down in front of the gateway, whilst holding one foot in his hand.

Sidgwick looked at me with startled eyes. Clearly Sherlock Holmes was a new experience for the drayman. 'Is he all right, Doctor?' he said, suspiciously.

'Mr Holmes is perfectly well,' I assured him.

Sidgwick said nothing more, but it was clear he was far from convinced.

'Watson.'

'Yes, Holmes.'

'You are a drayman. Please drive your horse along this lane and past the gateway.'

Like a child astride his hobby horse, I galloped along the roadway. As I reached the gateway, Holmes stopped hopping and fell headlong in front of me.

'Ha. It is exactly as I expected, Watson. The unfortunate Stamford fell in front of the dray whilst attempting to put on his other boot.'

The drayman, already half convinced of Holmes's insanity,

seemed now quite sure. He jumped aboard his dray and goaded the horse into action.

'If you want me further, gentlemen, I'll be found at the Spread Eagle until midday,' he cried, no doubt relieved to be rid of such peculiar companions as Holmes and myself.

It was by then nearly seven am. Young Onions was asked by Holmes to walk into the village and rouse the local constable. The remaining members of our little group returned to the house.

'You are quite certain about how poor Stamford met his death, Holmes?' I said.

'Indeed. It is quite clear to me that even if it was almost dark, he would hardly have simply walked out in front of the dray. There was nothing on the verge to indicate he might have tripped. It is plain enough. Stamford fell into the path of the dray, whilst attempting to put on his other boot.'

'But what on earth was he doing there at that time of the morning, and why was he dressed so strangely?'

'Well now, Doctor. Two or three possibilities occur to me, but without further information I cannot speculate.'

'What will you do now?'

'I shall more closely inspect the body of the late Stamford.'

'You expect to extract something more?'

'I do.'

We were met at the library door by a much agitated Lord Sheffield. He threw open the door and pointed to the space above the great fireplace.

'It is my painting. My Canaletto. It has been cut from its frame and stolen. This is quite, quite dreadful!'

Sherlock Holmes stepped lightly up onto the back of the

fireside chair and closely inspected the frame with the few remaining traces of canvas still adhering. 'This was the work of a man with a steady hand,' he said, running a long forefinger along the cut edge. 'The picture has been cut from its frame with no more than six strokes of what I should say is a very sharp blade. Indeed, it appears to be one that is surgically sharp.'

'A doctor's scalpel?' I hazarded.

'It has all the signs of being such an implement.'

'Could it be a medical man?'

Lord Sheffield snorted. 'That is of little assistance, Holmes. There are at this very moment at least sixteen medical men under this roof. Seventeen, if you count Watson here.'

Holmes jumped down. 'I did not say I believed the culprit to be a medical man. Indeed, my instincts are all against it.'

I pulled a face. 'That does not get us very far, Holmes. There are more than twenty guests in the house.'

Lord Sheffield was quite unimpressed. 'You are stating, Holmes, that despite the evidence pointing to the miscreant being a medical person, it was perpetrated by someone with no connection to the profession?'

'Exactly.'

'Then you are not the man I expected you to be. When the constable arrives, I shall point this matter out to him. Possibly he may be more clear sighted.'

Holmes gave a quick, thin smile. 'I am truly sorry if I have failed to rise to the standards your Lordship has expected from me.'

Lord Sheffield made no reply. He merely snorted and turned on his heel.

I took Holmes by the elbow and guided him in the

direction of the late Stamford's body.

'Well now, Holmes,' I said, as we crouched over the corpse. 'It seems to me we have two mysteries. Why was Stamford in the road and who purloined Lord Sheffield's painting?'

Holmes gave a brief smile. 'I believe his Lordship is drawing his own conclusions from these matters.' Sherlock Holmes said no more. He drew back the sheet and examined the clothing of the dead man.

'Hm. Empty pockets. Hello, look at this, Watson.'

'The trouser cuffs?'

'Indeed.'

I took one of the cuffs in my hand. 'Good heavens, it is soaking wet.'

'The other cuff is also wet.'

'But what does this mean, Holmes?'

'It means that early this morning, Stamford walked through a wet area on his way to the road.'

'He did not use the main path?'

'He did not.'

'Are you certain?'

'My dear Doctor, you, yourself, have just used the main path. Are your cuffs wet?'

I reached down and felt my trousers. 'Ah, no. But can you describe the route he did take?'

Holmes gave the matter a little thought. 'Yes, Doctor. I believe I can.'

Our conversation was halted by the arrival of a large red-faced constable. He was accompanied by Lord Sheffield, Price and the two students. 'Now, sir,' he said in his best official tone. 'I am Constable Turner. In the absence of an officer, I am in charge of this here investigation.'

'Good day, Constable,' said Holmes, in his artless way. 'If there is anything I can do to assist you in this matter, you have only to ask.'

'Thank you, sir,' said the constable huffily. 'I have heard from his Lordship all about your great powers of deduction. But I can assure you, Mr Holmes, this crime will be solved by good old-fashioned police work.'

Holmes bowed low. 'Then I leave you to your task.'

The constable asked several questions and took copious notes. 'Now, my Lord, we come to the stolen painting.'

'The Canaletto,' said Lord Sheffield.

'Now this painting, sir. Is it very valuable?'

Lord Sheffield seemed somewhat taken aback by the constable's ignorance. 'Yes, Constable. It is very valuable,' he said.

The policeman wrote again in his book. 'Now, sir, do you have any suspect or suspects in mind?'

Lord Sheffield glanced in our direction before answering. 'Yes, Constable, I believe so. I am of the opinion it was Foster Stamford, the man who is lying dead on the floor.'

I took a step forward. 'Surely, Lord Sheffield, you cannot believe that? Stamford was no thief.'

Lord Sheffield looked sadly at me. He spoke in a quiet and conciliatory tone. 'I am sorry, Watson. I understand that he was your friend, but when I think the matter over clearly, my accusation comes through a logical progression.

'At about five o'clock this morning, Stamford rose. He half dressed himself in order to be quickly able to undress again. He made his way downstairs to the library. Taking one of his scalpels, he jumped up on that very chair and cut the painting from the frame.

'Slipping outside, he made his way to the road where he

secreted the painting. I expect it will be discovered in the copse opposite the estate walls.

'His task completed, Stamford made to return to the house. Unfortunately, he stumbled and fell beneath the wheels of the passing dray, thereby preventing him from returning unnoticed to his bed.'

I shook my head and waved my hands at Lord Sheffield as if trying to push away the argument. 'No, no. I cannot believe it!'

Constable Turner spoke up. 'I must say, I'm inclined to agree, Dr Watson. Lord Sheffield has explained how the events came to pass. It seems to me that Mr Stamford is our man, right enough.'

Sherlock Holmes took me by the arm and led me away to the door. Onions rose from his seat as we passed by. 'Sorry, Dr Watson. I understand how you must feel. Old Stamford was a good sort. I cannot believe him to be a thief.'

Sherlock Holmes opened the library door and almost walked into Price, who had left the room quite unobserved by myself. He was carrying a large coffee tray. Suddenly Holmes gave me a tremendous shove which propelled me into the hallway with sufficient force to almost knock me off my feet. 'Watson,' he said, 'I must speak with you.'

I could feel a tingling vibration running up his arm. 'Holmes, what on earth is wrong?'

'Wrong? My dear fellow, there is nothing wrong. Indeed, nothing could be less wrong.'

Sherlock Holmes had dragged me as far as the garden before I was able to disentangle myself from his grip. 'Holmes, will you please tell me exactly what is going on?'

Holmes laughed. 'My dear Watson. Such a petulant face.' He looked around at the fine gardens. 'What a most pleasant morning. I believe there is time for a brisk walk before breakfast.'

By now I was almost exploding with frustration and ire, but Holmes was rapidly disappearing into the distance.

'Will you at least tell me where we are going?' I said, as we passed through the kitchen gardens.

'We are taking the route Stamford took this morning. The route, I might add, taken by the man he was following.'

At first I was dumbfounded by the revelation. It was then the events of a few minutes earlier came into my mind. 'Something occurred in the library which suggested to you that there was a second man.'

Holmes nodded. 'Indeed. It was a most singular event.'

'It was something to do with Price? Or perhaps it was young Onions, or maybe Mortimore?'

Holmes held up a stern forefinger. 'Not so fast, Doctor. Let us first cover the sequence of events.'

We had almost reached the boundary of the cricket ground. The pitch was laid out and the stumps were lying on the ground ready for action. In the middle distance were the three pavilions and in the far distance was the high wall which surrounded the estate.

Holmes was not interested in the pitch, nor was he bothered with the pavilions. Instead we kept to the long grass that skirted the ground and made our way to the wall.

I followed Holmes through a thicket of small trees. Then I saw the gateway. 'Why this is the very gate beside which poor Stamford was found.'

'It is.'

Holmes closely inspected the gate and the surrounding masonry. 'Ha! It is exactly as I expected,' he said. 'Look, Doctor. The ivy has been scraped away. You can see how the uncovered part of the door is more weather-beaten than the area around the lock which has been recently exposed.'

He knelt down and keenly scanned the lock mechanism. 'You will notice fresh scratches on the plate. Ah, oil,' he said, rubbing his forefinger and thumb together. 'This was no spur-of-the-moment crime, it was carefully planned.'

Holmes tried the door. It was securely locked. 'Well now,' he said, almost to himself. 'That is most suggestive.' He paused for a moment in reverie. 'By the way, Doctor. Will you quickly examine your trouser cuffs again for me?'

I bent down and felt the material. 'Good Lord, they are quite wet.'

Holmes smiled. 'Exactly, my dear Watson. Exactly.'

Sherlock Holmes rubbed his hands together and slapped me on the back. 'Come along, Watson. We have seen and done enough here, and breakfast is waiting.'

Breakfast at Sheffield Park was a sombre affair. Holmes had gone out, once more wishing to inspect the spot where poor Stamford had met his death. My appetite, usually robust, had withered away almost to nothing. A little toast was all I could manage.

Bonnor and Abel came in. They were quiet and subdued and spoke to each other in little more than whispers. Others, medical men and cricketers, moved about the room, but had little to say.

Then Singleton appeared at the door. 'Dr Watson. I have a message for you from Mr Holmes. Would you kindly meet him in Lord Sheffield's study in ten minutes?'

Finishing my coffee, I stood up, then walked across the dining room. The silence was almost deafening. I could almost feel every man's eyes on me and hear their silent opinions. 'There he goes, poor chap, who'd have thought his friend would turn out to be a thief.'

As I turned into the corridor which led to Lord Sheffield's study, I could hear raised voices from behind the door. Lord Sheffield was arguing with another man, whose voice I did not recognize.

I knocked at the door. It was Holmes, however, who answered. 'Come in, Watson.'

Lord Sheffield was sitting behind his desk. Holmes was perched upon the wide windowsill. The other occupant, a very large, dark-haired, moustached man, was standing by the desk.

Holmes slipped lightly from his seat. 'Ah, Watson. Permit me to introduce Inspector Harry Bullstrode. He has just arrived from East Grinstead.'

'Good day to you, Dr Watson,' he said briskly. 'Mr Holmes has acquainted me with all the facts. He has also convinced me that Mr Stamford was not the thief, which I expect you will be glad to hear.'

'Bullstrode has agreed to be part of a little deception I am arranging,' said Holmes, his eyes twinkling with amusement. 'It will mean, however, that the cricket match must go ahead.'

'If you think so . . .' I said, doubtfully. 'But I do not see . . .'

Lord Sheffield gave a snort. It was perfectly clear that he was against the idea. 'There has been an unsolved crime in my house and you wish to play cricket,' he roared. 'I do not understand you.'

'It is the only way I can uncloak the thief,' said Holmes.
'Then you know who the wretch is?'
'I do.'
'Then why do you not have him arrested immediately?'
'I have no concrete grounds. I could not recover the painting by having him arrested. Without it the police could not hold him.'
'Aye. That is so, sir,' said Bullstrode. 'We need the painting as evidence, and that's a fact.'
'If you desire to see your painting safely returned and the miscreant under lock and key, Lord Sheffield, you would do well to follow my advice,' said Holmes, flatly.
Lord Sheffield sat back in his chair and threw his hands up into the air in a gesture of defeat. 'Very well, Holmes,' he sighed. 'The match will commence at noon as originally intended.'
'Now, remember, Lord Sheffield,' said Holmes. 'You must say nothing of this matter to anyone. If you are questioned about your decision, you will merely say it was your view that as so many people had turned out to play, it would be unfair to deprive them of their day's sport.'
Lord Sheffield sighed again. 'Very well. I shall follow your instructions to the letter. But remember, Holmes, I expect this plan of yours to work.'
Sherlock Holmes smiled briefly, his eyes as hard as flint. 'It will, Lord Sheffield. It will.'

It was a little after noon when Holmes and I strolled across to the cricket ground. To observe the great detective, one would hardly have supposed him to be deeply involved in the deadly pursuit of a malefactor. He was once more dressed in his blazer and flannels and had completely adopted the mien of a holiday-making gentleman who is set for an afternoon's entertainment. Holmes had surprised all those present with his declaration of total belief in Stamford's guilt. Now he was creating the impression of complete indifference to the matter.

The ground looked splendid, decked out as it was in red, white and blue bunting and Union flags. The national banners of Australia and Canada were flying in celebration of George Bonnor and Charles Mortimore.

Close by to the Lord's Pavilion, a huge traction engine was thrumming and steaming. It produced the motive power for the music machine which was playing any number of stirring military marches and popular dance tunes. Resplendent also was the assembly of more than two hundred spectators: players, players' friends, friends and associates of Lord Sheffield, and village people, all enjoying the spectacle.

Everyone was full of enthusiasm and anticipation. So too was Sherlock Holmes, although his particular expectation was that of the hunter who lies in wait for an unsuspecting quarry.

The teams were led out of the Lord's Pavilion by Lord Sheffield. Down the steps they came, their whites gleaming in the sunshine.

Lord Sheffield's team won the toss and elected to bat. Abel and Singleton opened the innings, and began to score quickly against the inexperienced student bowlers. Abel took the score to 46 with a huge six that sailed over the pavilion.

'Excellent,' I cried.

Then Singleton was out. Clean bowled by Mortimore for 19. He was replaced by Reverend Mann, the local vicar. Again the score was quickly rattled up. Abel struck two more fours and the vicar cut and edged his way to 10, when he was caught in the slips off Onions. It was 77 for 2.

I turned to address Holmes. The heat of the day seemed to have made him doze off. Upon closer inspection, however, I observed him to be quite awake, his eyes glittering from beneath hooded lids.

'Are you watching the cricket, Holmes?'

'Hush, Watson. I am endeavouring to cultivate an air of supreme indifference to the whole of human activity.'

'What on earth do you mean?'

Sherlock Holmes raised his eyelids enough to look directly at me. He fixed me with a steely stare. 'It is quite simple, Doctor. I am seeking to allay the fears of the miscreant, who may yet be concerned for his safety. Although I have done much to that end, I cannot be seen to watch and observe the people around us intently for fear that I give my true game away. He is a clever fellow and doubtless realizes his peril. He can only relax if he is led to believe I am no longer interested in the matter.'

'You hope to catch him off his guard?'

'I do.'

'Ha,' I cried. 'How excellent.'

Gunn, the fast bowler came in. The brother of the Surrey all-rounder, he had little pretence to be a classical cricketer, but he had a strong arm, and dealt the medics some hefty blows. He soon disappeared, however, but not before smashing three huge sixes in his score of 32.

Baines, the young Cambridge Blue, came in to bat. Bonnor, who was padded up in readiness, strolled over and sat on the grass beside me.

'Hello, Doctor. I see Mr Holmes has dozed off. Is the cricket not to his liking?'

I laughed. 'No. But then again, sport, with perhaps the sole exception of pugilism, is not to his liking.'

Bonnor was not long delayed before it was his turn to bat. Baines missed an inswinging ball from Mortimore and was clean bowled for 3. The total was now 130 for 4.

The next few overs proved to be a complete nightmare for the medical men, as Bonnor put their bowlers to the sword. The final ten overs of the innings cost them 128 runs as the young giant scored 86. Abel added a further 40 which took his score to 101 not out and Lord Sheffield's team to 258 for 4.

Lord Sheffield met his two batsmen on the pavilion steps. He slapped them on the back. 'Well done,' he cried. 'Well played, Bonnor. I made it eighty-six off thirty-eight balls.'

They disappeared into the pavilion, followed by their team mates and the men of the medical school.

All about us were the signs of hampers being unpacked and tea things being set out on rugs. Behind us the traction engine chugged into life again and, as before, the mechanical band began to play.

Sherlock Holmes pushed back his boater and reached for his watch. He flipped open the case and gave a quick smile. 'Ah. It is time.'

I looked up from my cold beef and pickles. 'Time, my dear fellow? Time for what?'

Holmes sat up quite straight and looked back towards the house. My eye followed the direction of his gaze. A plump figure was running in our direction. It was a footman from the house.

'Where is his Lordship?' he demanded.

Holmes gave a quick smile and stood up. 'What is it? What has happened?'

'It is the house,' cried the footman. 'It is on fire.'

A young fellow sitting not very far from Holmes and myself, suddenly stood up and pointed to the house. 'Look,' he said. 'Smoke.'

Holmes was immediately galvanized into action. 'Fire. Fire,' he cried. 'Sheffield House is on fire.'

Lord Sheffield appeared at the pavilion door. 'Quickly,' he shouted. 'We must get to the house.'

I rose to join the throng which was rapidly making its way to the house, but Holmes took me firmly by the arm. I could feel that he was laughing.

'What is happening? Why are we delaying?'

'We are delaying, Doctor, because we are awaiting the arrival of the miscreant. One way or another he will use this timely diversion to obtain his hidden spoils and escape with them. Of that, I have no doubt.'

'But what of the fire?'

'There is no fire.'

Holmes stiffened and pulled me down behind the picnicking table used by the friends of Singleton. 'We are in luck,' he whispered. 'It is our man.'

'You are certain?'

'Indeed. Who else would be departing the scene of a fire?'

I looked up to see over the table, but Holmes pulled me down again. I heard him grunt. 'Hm. This is most interesting, Watson. He appears to be empty handed.'

'You are surprised?'

'Not entirely.'

Holmes stood up. He pulled me to my feet. 'Come, Watson. We cannot delay.'

'But where are we going?'

Instead of replying, Holmes began to run. At first I expected him to make for one of the pavilions in an attempt to intercept his man. I was surprised to see him, however, making for the small copse and the little gateway beyond.

After several moments of hard running, Sherlock Holmes and I crashed through the thicket and into the small clearing beyond. For a few seconds, I stood there in the sunshine, attempting to regain my breath.

'Watson,' Holmes hissed. 'For pity's sake, man, get yourself out of sight. Our man will be upon us at any moment.'

I ducked quickly into the deep recess in the wall which surrounded the gateway. It was an action taken none too soon, for within seconds I heard the sound of running feet.

Cautiously, I looked out from my place of concealment. A dark-haired man with his back to me laid down the bundle he was carrying and pulled a large key from his trouser pocket. There was a sharp click as the mechanism operated, and a creak as the old door opened.

It was then, when Sherlock Holmes sprang from his hiding place and seized at the man. For a few moments they struggled. Then Holmes tripped his man and sent him crashing to the ground. 'Now, Mr Harold Price. I have you.'

'Price?' I cried.

'Indeed,' said Sherlock Holmes calmly.

Price lay inertly on the grass, his face white with rage and consternation. Holmes, who held his prisoner in a vice-like grip, smiled coldly at me. 'My dear Watson. Will you do me a small service?'

'Certainly, if I am able.'

'Will you tell Harry Bullstrode he may now take Mr Price away?'

I cried out for the inspector. The door was pushed fully open and Bullstrode stood there, his large frame almost filling the opening. He gave a signal to the two constables in the road, who swiftly relieved Holmes of his burden.

'Good work, Mr Holmes,' he said.

Price struggled with his captors and, for a brief moment, he forced them to turn back again. The inspector glared at the miscreant. 'Come quietly now, Price, or it will be the worse for you.'

Price glared at the policeman, but he made no further attempt to resist. He merely snorted a threat. 'You have not heard the last of me, Mr Sherlock Holmes. One day I shall return and Lord Sheffield will rue the day he allowed you to interfere in my affairs.'

Then he was gone.

As Sherlock Holmes and I returned to the house, we were met by an exasperated Lord Sheffield. 'It was all a hoax,' he cried. 'Some idiot set off smoke bombs in the attic. There will be repercussions for this, I can assure you.'

His Lordship turned and gazed about him. 'Price. Price! Where the devil is the fellow? He is never around when I want him.'

Sherlock Holmes gave a sharp smile. 'Mr Price is presently in custody. By now he should be well on his way to East Grinstead police station.'

'I do not understand. Price is in the hands of the police?'

'Indeed.'

Holmes, his face a veritable tableau of supreme self-satisfaction, removed the rolled-up painting from its place of hiding behind his back and unfurled it on the ground before the feet of an astonished Lord Sheffield.

'Good Lord. My Canaletto.'

George Bonnor stepped forward from the growing crowd and gave Sherlock Holmes a hearty slap on the back. 'Congratulations, Mr Holmes,' he cried.

For a moment, Lord Sheffield stood and surveyed his Canaletto. Then he began to laugh. 'Very well done, sir,' he cried, taking Holmes by the hand. 'You have exceeded all my expectations. Indeed you have, sir. Price, the thief, eh?'

Onions grasped Holmes by the arm. 'Good work, sir. You must tell us how you came to achieve this remarkable feat.'

There came several murmurs of agreement. Holmes, however, held up his hand. 'Gentlemen. You forget. There is a cricket match in progress. The game must be played to its conclusion.'

Of the cricket match, there remains little to tell. The medical team were utterly outclassed by Lord Sheffield's XI.

Onions and the Hon. Chesney Blythe opened the innings, but were soon removed by Alf Shaw with only 10 on the board. Three more wickets fell and the students who came in scored a mere 52. Then Mortimore came in and scored a bright 28 before he was LBW to Bonnor. Three more wickets fell, two of them to Bonnor, and there was stout resistance by Wilson, who smashed four fours in a brave innings of 19. He was the last man out, when he was caught by Abel off Bonnor, who finished with 4 for 38 to add to his innings of 86. The medics were all out for 142 and Lord Sheffield's XI were the victors by 116 runs.

Supper was a hearty affair. Many appetites, including that of John H. Watson, MD, had undergone a remarkable improvement. It was only when the inner man had been fortified and each had settled down for a smoke and a glass that cheers, that Sherlock Holmes was prepared to reveal the plan by which he had ensnared Harold Price.

Sherlock Holmes, his pipe freshly charged, a large brandy by his elbow, lay back in the generous armchair. About him, like the court of some great Mogul emperor, sat every man jack who had been involved in the day's activities.

Lord Sheffield sipped his drink and looked at Holmes. 'Now, come along, my dear fellow. You have kept us in suspense for quite long enough.'

'Yes, indeed, Mr Holmes,' said Abel. 'You must tell us how you unmasked that bounder, Price.'

'Well now,' said Holmes, evenly, 'let us return to the very first incident this morning. When Stamford was so tragically run down in the road. Was that incident alone not a pretty mystery?'

'It was indeed,' said his Lordship, in tones of some embarrassment. 'When I discovered my Canaletto was missing, I believed the mystery had been solved.'

Holmes smiled. 'It took only the quickest of glances at the empty frame to see it could not possibly be the work of Stamford.'

'But how so? The material was cut by a clinical blade. I seem to recall you remarking upon the neatness of the work.'

'That is so,' I said. 'It was clearly the work of a medical man.'

'Incorrect, Watson. It was seemingly the work of a medical man. Medical men do not make long slashes, they are used to making small neat cuts.'

'That could still not exclude Stamford from the list of suspects.'

'My dear Watson, that is where you are precisely wrong. Your conversation with Stamford, which I overheard, proved as much to me.'

'Of course,' I said, seeing the light at last. 'Stamford had to retire because of the after-effects of enteric fever. His hands had become so shaky, he could no longer practice his speciality.'

'Exactly. He could never have made such a fine job of it.'

'Excellent,' I cried.

Holmes took another pull at his pipe and surveyed the audience with keen eyes. Bonnor cleared his throat. 'But that did not exclude the possibility of Mr Stamford being an accomplice to the actual thief.'

'No, indeed. It was a possibility which immediately occurred to me,' said Holmes. 'It was, however, the strange manner in which Stamford was dressed which convinced me that this was an unlikely scenario.'

Holmes turned again to look at me. 'Watson, you will recall certain remarks I made at the time.'

'Indeed. But I am sorry to say I could not make head or tail of them.'

'Ah, well. No matter.' Holmes leaned forward and laid down his pipe. 'Firstly, there was the matter of Stamford's general appearance. He was wearing odd clothes. He was also without socks and had on only one boot. He was hardly dressed for roaming all over the grounds of Shef-field Park.'

'Of course,' I cried. 'Stamford indicated that he was a chronic insomniac. At five am he was awake, but still dressed for sleep.'

'Exactly. Possibly he was up and about looking for a book to read, or seeking a drink of water when he was disturbed by the thief. In all probability he observed the miscreant making a rapid exit from the library with a large bundle tucked under his arm. Upon investigation he saw the Canaletto had been cut down from its frame. Realizing that the thief was making his escape, he swiftly returned to his room. Throwing on the first clothes that came to hand and carrying his boots, he ran as hard as he was able in pursuit of the thief.'

'Who was making an exit across the cricket ground,' I added.

'No, Watson. He made his exit around the cricket ground.'

I nodded in recognition. 'It was the exact route you and I took earlier today.'

Lord Sheffield looked puzzled. 'But how were you able to conclude that the path of Stamford and Price led around the cricket ground?'

Holmes smiled. I also knew the answer. 'It was because of Stamford's wet trouser cuffs,' I said. 'They were wet from the dew.'

'Indeed?'

'Thank you, Watson,' said Holmes, a trifle icily. 'I had earlier observed that all other routes were dry. The main pathway is gravel and rather dusty and the direct route across the cricket ground with its regularly mown grass would have made only his feet wet.'

Abel looked troubled. 'Could Stamford get his cuffs wet from the grass verges, Mr Holmes?'

'An excellent question, Mr Abel. The answer is no. The verges had been cut quite short too. The route around the cricket ground was the only one possible.'

'But why did Stamford not stop to put on his boots?' asked Bonnor.

'Quite simply, because he did not have the opportunity

to do so,' said Holmes. 'Indeed, it was not until he reached the road that he first came to put on one boot.

'Possibly Stamford saw Price exit into the road and stop for a moment whilst he selected a suitable site to secrete his ill-gotten gains. Stamford, I have no doubt, took this opportunity to get one boot on. It was when he tried to get his other boot on, that he lost his balance and fell into the road.'

'And right under the wheels of a passing dray. Poor fellow,' said Onions.

'But the drayman reported nothing of the presence of another person in the road,' said Abel, thoughtfully.

'No, indeed,' said Holmes. 'His mind, fully taken up by the dreadful accident, would allow him little opportunity for observing peripheral events.'

'Then Price was able to slip back through the gateway quite unnoticed,' I said.

'Exactly.'

Holmes emptied his glass and set it down on the table beside him.

'Can you say if Price was intending to make off with the painting, Mr Holmes, or was he just meaning to hide it?' said Lord Sheffield.

'I believe it was the latter,' Holmes replied. 'If Price had disappeared at the same time as your painting, you would have undoubtedly had the forces of law and order on his heels within hours.'

'Then Price returned to the estate, still in possession of his ill-gotten gains?' I said.

'Just so. He relocked the gate and left Stamford to his fate. You will also recall, Watson, that the very fact the gate was locked gave rise to my considerable interest.'

'Indeed. But I fail to understand why.'

Sherlock Holmes sighed and drummed his fingers on the arm of his chair. 'Because, Doctor, it reinforced the innocence of Stamford. You will recall that the gate has a large locking mechanism which entails the need for a similarly robust key. Yet no key of any kind was found on the body, nor yet anywhere in or nearby the road. This clearly indicated the presence of a second individual.'

'Exactly,' I said. 'Stamford would have hardly locked the gate if he was intending to immediately return.'

Holmes grunted. 'It is even more unlikely that, like Lazarus, he would have risen, relocked the gate, like some magician made the key vanish, then return to a comatose state.'

'The drayman would certainly have noticed such an event and reported it,' said Bonnor.

Holmes carefully refilled his pipe before continuing. 'Price was in something of a quandary. He realized that it would be only a matter of minutes before the alarm was raised. At that very moment the drayman was doubtless on his way to the house to report the accident.

'He had to make a snap decision. He had to take one of two options. He could take the painting back to the house and run the risk of apprehension, or he could hide it in a more convenient hole.'

'One of the pavilions,' I said.

'Indeed. There was, of course, the small risk of the painting coming to light during the cricket match. There was, however, little choice. He slipped the bundle into a convenient niche and quickly returned to the house, where he endeavoured to act as if nothing had occurred.'

Lord Sheffield slapped his knee. 'Damned fellow!'

'This is all excellent stuff, Holmes,' I said. 'The pieces fit as well as those in any jigsaw. But one piece remains missing.'

'The clue which confirmed Price's guilt?'

'Exactly, Holmes. I believe I know when you discovered it, but I do not know what the clue was.'

Holmes smiled a little. 'As you will recall, Doctor, when Stamford's body was brought up to the house, I examined it and I discovered his trousers had wet cuffs.'

'Yes, of course. You have made much of that point, but I still do not understand.'

'You will also recall that very soon afterwards the room became filled with concerned people.'

'I do.'

'It was then I noticed one other with wet trouser cuffs. It was Price. From the very moment he entered the room I noticed that the bottoms of his light grey flannels were several shades darker than the rest of the material. Clearly, he was my man. Who else but someone intimately involved in the theft of the painting could have trouser cuffs so affected?'

'Excellent,' I cried. 'The final piece of the jigsaw. It all fits together quite beautifully. Holmes, you are to be congratulated.'

There came a murmur of assent from the assembly. This was swiftly followed by a round of applause, led by Bonnor and Abel.

Lord Sheffield stood up and joined in the clapping. He then held out his hand to Holmes who also rose, only to find himself almost crushed in a warm embrace. His Lordship's eye was moist and his voice cracked with emotion. 'You have saved my Canaletto. My pride and joy. Thank you, Sherlock Holmes.'

It was late on Sunday afternoon when Holmes and I spoke once again about the events of Saturday. We were sitting quietly in a first-class smoker on the London-bound train. I was making up my notes into a form which could be quickly absorbed, if in the future Holmes needed them for reference.

'Holmes.'

'Yes, my dear fellow.'

'There is one question about the events of yesterday, which occurs to me.'

'If I can be of any assistance.'

'Why do you suppose Price should choose the very weekend that Sheffield Park would be simply crawling with people, to purloin his Lordship's painting?'

Holmes tapped the ash from his cigarette. 'There is safety in numbers, Watson. The greater the number, the greater the number of suspects.'

'It was a factor which also worked against him,' I said. 'Because of his insomnia, poor Stamford was wandering around the house at the time.'

'Watson.'

'Yes, Holmes?'

'Perhaps you should immediately publish this narrative. It will serve as an excellent obituary for Stamford. It will be a testament to his bravery and unselfishness in attempting to protect the property of a friend from the evil machinations of a vile wretch, who cared only for his own selfish ends.'

I leaned forward and slapped my knee.

'And so it will,' I cried. 'For I shall begin the account the very moment we reach Baker Street.'

In fond memory of
Foster Stamford, MD, FRCS
1855–1896
RIP

The Irish Professor

The year of 1897 saw Sherlock Holmes mine a particularly rich seam of success. Thumbing through my scrapbook, I am reminded of the events surrounding Professor Hugo O'Neill. Events which were to lead Sherlock Holmes to cross four countries and entangle one of Ireland's finest families in a web of heroic deceptions, before Holmes finally laid his man by the heels.

It was during the spring of the year. I had recently closed my old practice and was waiting for my new one to become ready. As a temporary measure I was acting as a locum for my colleague, Jackson, at his practice in Belmont Square.

There was a tap at the consulting room door and Jenny, the maid, appeared. 'Your last patient, Dr Watson. Mr O'Neill.'

'Ah yes, he is to have some stitches out.'

'Yes, sir.'

'Send him in, please.'

A moment later a tall broad-shouldered man strode through the door. He was a man I instantly recognized.

'Hugo O'Neill,' I cried. 'My dear fellow.'

'Hello, John. How are you?'

Mr O'Neill was none other than the celebrated Irish mathematician Professor Hugo O'Neill, late of University

College Dublin, with whom as a schoolboy I had once been fortunate enough to share a study.

'Apart from these stitches which are to be removed, I am fine,' he said, warmly, shaking my proffered hand.

'I had no idea you were in London.'

'It was necessary to come. I had a conference to attend and a seminar to give.'

'Are you staying for long?'

'I will be in London for three more days, then I am to return to Ireland for a much-needed holiday.'

I took up my instruments and attended to O'Neill's stitches. There were three in his forehead.

'How did you come by these?' I said. O'Neill laughed. 'It was all because of a pickpocket. In my attempt to apprehend the miscreant, I fell and cracked my head. It was fortunate that I just so happened to be in this very square when the accident occurred. Dr Jackson took me in immediately and repaired the damage.'

'A most regrettable incident,' I said. 'I think, however, that there should be no scar.'

O'Neill laughed again. 'Perhaps I shall be less lucky on the next occasion.'

'What on earth do you mean, O'Neill? Are you expecting another such incident?'

'It is the second occasion when some villain has attempted to rob me,' he said. 'As it is often stated that things occur in threes, I can only expect another such event.'

'What of the first incident?' I said.

'It occurred on the second day after my arrival in London. I was returning to my hotel room when a man almost knocked me down. Fortunately, I was assisted by a clerical gentleman who returned to me my stolen wallet the fellow had lifted, quite without my knowledge.'

'Did you inform the police?'

'No. I had my wallet and there seemed to be no harm done. Now, however, I am beginning to wonder if it would not be wise to do so.'

'Perhaps,' I said. 'I might introduce you to another agency, someone of far greater perspicacity than our rather obtuse police force?'

O'Neill gave me a slightly puzzled look. 'Of course, John, if you judge it pertinent. But who is this genius you wish me to consult?'

I smiled. 'He is Sherlock Holmes.'

Sherlock Holmes was perched upon his chair, his legs drawn up and his hands clasped around his knees. So deep in reverie was he that our arrival occurred completely unnoticed by him.

After a few moments Holmes became aware of our presence. 'Ah, Watson, please accept my apologies, but there is presently something of great importance on my mind.'

'You have a new case?'

'Indeed, Doctor, a particularly abstruse and complicated matter which will require me to immediately leave for France.'

'You are leaving tonight?'

'I have ordered a cab to be here by eight pm.'

'Well, Holmes, this is news indeed. I had hoped that you might be able to assist my friend, O'Neill.'

Holmes took out his watch and scanned it. 'Any friend of yours, Watson. Good evening, O'Neill. How may I be of assistance to you?'

Briefly, O'Neill recounted his experiences to Sherlock Holmes.

'Well now, Professor, you do seem to have been uncommonly unfortunate in your short stay.'

O'Neill smiled. 'Indeed, Mr Holmes, it would almost seem as if someone had organized a welcoming committee for me.'

O'Neill and I began to laugh at his jest, but I was almost immediately silenced by the most peculiar look which had come over the face of Sherlock Holmes. It was, however, replaced in an instant by a quick smile.

'I would not over-concern yourself, Professor. The common pickpocket is not a dangerous fellow, but as you have sought my advice, I will freely give you some. Keep away from doctors with over-active imaginations.'

It was past nine pm. Sherlock Holmes was by now well on his way to Dover. O'Neill had willingly stayed for supper and we had spent a pleasurable evening recalling past boyhood adventures. All too soon, however, he announced that he would have to be getting back to his hotel. I helped O'Neill on with his coat.

'Listen, John, you are at something of a loose end, are you not? Your new practice will not be ready for a month and Mr Holmes is to be away for goodness knows how long. What would you say to joining me for a week or so in Ireland? I have rented a cottage near Sligo Town and there would be more than enough room for two.'

I smiled and raised my glass in salute. 'My dear Hugo, I would love to come.'

It was four am, on the first of June. A heavy mist hung over the port of Liverpool. The *Dunlaghaire* was to be our ferryboat. Despite the early hour, the docks were a hive of activity. Little cranes, their jibs rising and falling, loading and unloading the cargo which had come from and was going to Ireland. Dockers, their muscles straining with effort, were piling up and unpiling the containers, and dozens of passengers were embarking and disembarking.

'Here we are, John,' said O'Neill. 'Here is the gangway. We had better hurry, though. She sails in half an hour.'

O'Neill and I quickly found our cabins and were soon strolling on the deck. The cables were released and we were under way.

Among our companions was a tall willowy young woman. She was quite beautifully attired in a long dress and coat. Suddenly, her handbag slipped from her grasp.

'Allow me, miss,' said O'Neill, as he retrieved the lady's bag.

'Thank you, sir,' she said, in a light sparkling voice.

'Forgive the familiarity,' said O'Neill, 'but may I introduce myself and my companion. This is Dr John Watson and I am Hugo O'Neill.'

The lady laughed. 'Professor O'Neill, I believe. An eminent gentleman, I am told. I am Miss Noel.'

I bowed slightly. 'A pleasure.'

'Good day, Dr Watson. Tell me, can you be the same Dr Watson who has so excellently recounted the activities of Sherlock Holmes?'

O'Neill laughed. 'Our fame precedes us, John.'

'Perhaps Miss Noel will join us for breakfast?' I said. 'Assuming that the exalted air we exude would not be too great a tax on her constitution.'

Miss Noel laughed again. 'It would be a pleasure, Dr

Watson. Just allow me to remain adjacent to an open window, please.'

Some four hours later as our ship docked in Dublin, Miss Noel shook hands with O'Neill and myself, then took her leave.

'If you will secure us a cab, John, I will collect our luggage,' said O'Neill.

'Very well,' I said. 'Are we, however, to make for the station?'

'My dear fellow, you Londoners are always in such a rush. I intend to show you something of my City of Dublin before we leave for Sligo.'

'Cab, sir?' said a tall, dark-haired man with mutton-chop whiskers.

'Thank you,' I said as he gave a loud whistle.

A four-wheeler drew up. The driver, a short thick-set man wearing a billycock hat, leaped from his seat and bowed low.

'Ah, there you are,' cried O'Neill. 'Good man, John. Here, help me with the bags.'

The driver and O'Neill began loading bags into the carriage. The man with the mutton-chop whiskers helped me lift the trunk. Suddenly O'Neill was tipped over by mutton-chops.

'Look out, John,' he cried. 'The fellow has my bag.'

The man was quickly making his escape in the direction of the river.

'Stop, thief,' I cried, running after the man.

Several faces were turned in my direction. As we turned towards Baggott Street, a tall man with a goatee beard, blocked the miscreant's way. There was a brief struggle and mutton-chops was apprehended.

'Hold him, sir.'

The man chuckled. 'Be assured, sir, the fellow cannot escape me. Is this your bag?'

'It is my friend's.'

The man smiled grimly. 'Then take it, sir, whilst I ensure that this fellow gets his just deserts.'

'Your name, sir?' I cried, as my benefactor dragged away his prisoner. 'Who am I to thank?'

'Taffe,' he said. 'Michael Taffe.'

'Thank you, Mr Taffe,' I said, but he had already gone.

Later O'Neill showed me the sights of Dublin: the General Post Office, the River Liffey, the Cathedral, the Castle and, of course, University College, where we lunched. By two pm we were on a train bound for Sligo with a change to a local service at Carrick on Shannon.

The day had become both warm and humid. My eyes, wearied by the hours of travel, began to close and before very long I was asleep.

There was a cessation in motion and doors were slamming. I opened my eyes with a jerk. O'Neill was sitting opposite, smiling. 'Ah, Rip Van Winkle, I presume.'

'Sorry, old man,' I said, blinking around me. 'Where are we?'

'Longford. The train stops here for fifteen minutes.'

'Perhaps I will get out and stretch my legs.'

The station was busy with the traffic of people and luggage. Then a warning whistle was blown and we were off again. I sat back to read the newspaper I had purchased. The wind, however, blew it about rather badly.

'Hugo,' I murmured, 'would you mind lifting the window.'

The strap was a little stiff and O'Neill put his head through the window to see what was causing the obstruction. 'Good Lord!'

'Something wrong?'

'That man who accosted the villain that stole my bag,' he said.

'What about him?'

'He has just come running down the platform and jumped aboard the train.'

'Carrick on Shannon, this is Carrick on Shannon,' the metallic voice of the station announcer boomed across the platform. O'Neill disappeared in the direction of the baggage car. Of Mr Taffe, the man seen by O'Neill, there was no sign.

Moments later, O'Neill reappeared. He was followed by a porter. He looked a little perplexed. 'John, old man,' he said. 'Part of your luggage seems to be missing. I believe it is the Gladstone bag.'

'Excuse me, sir,' said the porter. 'Perhaps you left it off in Dublin, or it was taken off by mistake at Longford. I will ask the station master to telegraph.'

'If you would be so kind,' I said, rather peevishly.

'Poor old John,' said O'Neill. 'This holiday is turning into quite a trial of endurance.'

Events, however, were to conspire to make life even more difficult. We were informed that there were no trains to Sligo. Any further progress would have to be made by carriage.

A four-wheeler was eventually engaged. Soon we were bowling along the lanes of County Roscommon.

'Does it not occur to you, Hugo,' I said, 'that there is something rather peculiar happening?'

'What on earth do you mean?'

'Well, ever since your arrival in London, you have been the victim of crime. When you return to Ireland, a similar set of circumstances prevail. Could it be that you have in your possession something of value?'

'If I have, then I cannot imagine what it might be.'

'You will agree that there is something more to these events than simple coincidence.'

'It seems highly probable,' said O'Neill. 'But do not forget it was your bag that has been stolen, if indeed it has not simply been lost in transit.'

I sighed. 'That is so, but perhaps my bag was taken in mistake for yours. All Gladstone bags look rather similar.'

'But what about this man, Taffe?'

'Yes, I had quite forgotten about him,' I said.

'It is all beyond me, John.'

'Indeed, I just wish that Holmes were here with us.'

Eventually, we arrived in Sligo. The key to O'Neill's cottage was in the hands of Father MacManus. I reigned the horses in and O'Neill jumped down. The priest, a small white-haired man of indeterminate years, greeted us cordially, then sent us on our way with clear instructions for the road to Knocknarea. On the way I stopped off at Bolands, a gentleman's outfitters in Wine Street, to purchase a few replacements for my missing things.

The green rolling countryside and the fresh salty air proved to be a great tonic. More than once I thought of Sherlock Holmes and his aversion to any air not already contaminated by the streets of London, and I also wondered if he was any nearer to solving the case which had taken him to the Continent.

On the second morning, O'Neill led me on a walk through the country lanes, through the village of Strandhill and up Knocknarea, the highest point south of Sligo Town. At the top we discovered the cairn that covered the tomb of Queen

Maeve, an ancient Irish chieftain's daughter.

The land spread out below us like a beautiful painting. To our left was the town of Sligo and beyond it lay Ben Bulbin with its peculiarly flat top and nose almost sticking into the sea. To our right were the lakes or loughs, including Lough Gill, and below were the fields with crops of potatoes, wheat and barley.

I took a deep breath, 'Wonderful!'

O'Neill nodded. 'Yes, indeed.'

From below came the sound of shots being fired.

'Someone catching their supper,' remarked O'Neill.

Suddenly there was a ping sound and a large chip flew away from the rock. There was a cry of pain from my companion.

'Hugo, what has happened?'

'I think a piece of that blasted rock has lodged itself in my eye.'

'Here, let me look.'

Even the most perfunctory inspection was sufficient to ascertain that O'Neill was correct. A small fragment of rock was lodged in his eyeball.

'We must try and find a local doctor,' I said. 'Instruments are required to remove the splinter.'

'I believe there is a doctor in Strandhill,' said O'Neill.

'Hold this handkerchief over your eye, old man, and try not to move your eye too much or to rub it,' I said.

In Strandhill we were overtaken by a man on horseback.

'Excuse me, sir. Can you tell me where the doctor lives? My friend has been hurt.'

The rider, a bearded, somewhat severe, portly man of about forty, reined his horse in. 'Is that you, Hugo?' he said. 'What has happened?'

'Captain Grey-Wynn,' said O'Neill. 'Is it you? My friend, Watson, and I were up near Maeve's tomb. We heard some shooting. I expect it was a local man after his supper. Then a stray bullet hit a stone and a chip flew off into my eye.'

'Probably some blasted poacher who thought I wasn't around,' growled Captain Grey-Wynn.

Fortunately for O'Neill, the doctor's house was nearby and the splinter was quickly removed. His eye suffered little damage and only required some drops which the doctor supplied.

Captain Grey-Wynn walked his horse back with us to the cottage. As we walked, O'Neill told the captain of our various adventures both in England and in Ireland.

The captain laughed, 'Whither Sherlock Holmes?'

'Whither, indeed,' I said, with great feeling.

The next morning I took a walk into the village to purchase a newspaper and some pipe tobacco. A four-wheeler containing two passengers came rattling along towards me.

'Good morning, Dr Watson. How are you today?'

It was the voice of Captain Grey-Wynn. Beside him sat a sharp-featured young man with a drooping moustache.

'Good morning, Captain. I am well,' I replied.

'I do not believe you have met my cousin, Sir Josslyn Gore-Booth,' said the Captain.

'Good day, Dr Watson. How do you like our country?' said Sir Josslyn.

'I like it a great deal.'

'You will visit Glencar and Ben Bulbin?'

'Indeed. Hugo and I are planning to go this afternoon.'

'Capital,' said Sir Josslyn. 'Perhaps you will both honour us with your presence at Lissadell tonight. We are having an evening soirée. You will find us nearby to your afternoon excursion.'

I bowed. 'Thank you, it would be a pleasure.'

The afternoon sun blazed down on our heads and the cool damp air that surrounded the waterfall at Glencar came as a great relief. O'Neill, whose eye was still a little sore, bathed his face in the cold water.

Suddenly there was a movement in the bushes behind me. A tall blond man stood there, his blue eyes cold and metallic, were fixed on O'Neill's back. Slowly his hand was raised. He had a silver revolver, and it was aimed at O'Neill.

'Hugo,' I cried, throwing myself at the man. 'Look out!'

The man gave an involuntary start. It was clear that he had not observed my presence. There was a loud bang in my ear as the revolver exploded into life. The hot blast of the charge was on my cheek and the smell of cordite was in my nostrils.

In an instant the man had broken free of my grip, like a startled rabbit he ran. My senses were too scattered to restrain him. There was a crashing through the undergrowth and he was gone.

O'Neill dragged me to my feet. 'John, are you hurt?'

I gave a weak smile. 'There is no need to concern yourself, old fellow. The gunshot quite missed me.'

'Because of you, it missed me too,' he said, gathering up his things. 'This has all gone too far. I must inform the police.'

Minutes later we were tramping down the road to Drumcliffe when a rider came upon us at great speed. He hardly seemed to notice our presence, as he made no attempt to rein his horse in. An instant later he was gone.

'Good heavens, Hugo, did you observe who the rider was?' I said.

'Indeed. It was Taffe.'

It had proved to be a fortunate coincidence that when O'Neill and I had stabled our horse and trap in Drumcliffe earlier in the afternoon, I had noticed the presence of a local constable. When after almost an hour's walking, we returned to the village, we were soon to be the recipients of good fortune, when we encountered the very man whom we were seeking.

'It will have to be reported to headquarters in Sligo Town,' said the constable, gloomily. 'I expect it will have to go to Dublin as well.'

O'Neill smiled at me. 'Well, John, are you enjoying Ireland?'

The day had been an eventful one. Indeed, there had been incidents aplenty during my short reacquaintance with O'Neill. Events which would have greatly interested Sherlock Holmes. Not for the first time did I wish him to be at hand.

As O'Neill and I drove along the dusty lanes between Drumcliffe and Lissadell House, we attempted to piece together the events of the last few days. As Holmes had so often remonstrated with his clients, 'The facts, give me the facts.'

I resolved to copy his methods. 'Let us go over the incidents together,' I said. 'You arrived in London ten days ago.'

'That is correct.'

'You have visited London before?'

'Many times.'

'You have never been the victim of violence before?'

'Never.'

'And here in Ireland?'

'Never.'

I stopped and thought for a moment. 'On this occasion, had you any special engagements?'

'No, it was very much as usual. There was a meeting of mathematicians at the Guildhall. I then gave a seminar on geometrics at University College. It is a reciprocal event with my own University College in Dublin.'

'There was nothing unusual happening during or after these events?'

'Not at all. I saw nothing but the same old faces I had seen for many a year.'

'Then you have not received any valuables to bring back with you?'

'No, not unless you count this stick pin given to me by Mr George Moore as of any great worth.'

O'Neill pulled a small pin from his tie. 'I believe it is made of jet, but I do not think that it is particularly valuable.'

'But the attacks continue, each more desperate,' I said. 'It is certain that someone thinks you have returned to Ireland with something of great value in your possession.'

'It is a total mystery to me,' said O'Neill.

I sighed, 'As it also is to me.'

Our conversation was abruptly interrupted by a salute given to us by an elderly gentleman riding a white horse. As he drew a little nearer, I saw that he was dressed in clerical garb. 'Good evening, gentlemen,' he said. 'Am I to assume that you are calling at Lissadell House?'

'Indeed we are, sir,' I said.

'Then we shall be travelling companions over the short distance that remains.' He pulled his horse a little closer. 'Permit me to introduce myself. I am the Reverend Le-Fanu, the Anglican Minister hereabouts.'

We rattled on down the leafy lanes which were by now becoming quite dark. Then I saw for the first time Lissadell House. The whole place was lit up like fairyland. The lawn which ran down to the sea was festooned with tall poles from which lanterns had been hung. Dozens of people were moving about, casting giant shadows, and the sound of Irish music filled the air.

\ The Reverend Le-Fanu was clearly a well-known and respected visitor. The staff, although pleasant enough to O'Neill and myself, greeted him with cordiality. We were shown through to the garden.

'My dear Reverend and Professor O'Neill and Dr Watson.' Sir Josslyn had detached himself from a small party of friends. 'Thank you for coming. I am sorry father cannot be here to greet you, but he is somewhere in Greenland, I believe.'

'I trust that he did not depart because he knew we were coming,' said O'Neill.

Sir Josslyn laughed. 'Not at all, Hugo; this trip has been planned for many months. He is hoping to experience the midnight sun.'

'Good Lord,' said O'Neill.

'Yes,' I said. 'I have read about that above a certain latitude the sun never sets in the summer months.'

Sir Josslyn led us across the lawn. 'You must meet what's left of my family. Mother, this is Dr Watson and Professor O'Neill, the Reverend is here also.'

Lady Gore-Booth held out a fine yet firm hand. 'Gentlemen, my son has told me a great deal about your adventures here in Sligo.'

'Mother,' said Sir Josslyn, 'where is my sister?'

Lady Gore-Booth pointed out a tall young woman half-hidden in the shade of an awning. Sir Josslyn immediately called out to her, 'Con!'

'My daughter, Constance,' said Lady Gore-Booth. 'Unfortunately, my other daughter, Eva, is presently in Manchester, so cannot be with us tonight.'

O'Neill and I looked at each other as Constance Gore-Booth walked into the light.

'Miss Noel,' I said.

'Dr Watson,' she said, sweetly, 'How nice to see you again.'

'But, how, what?' said O'Neill, in some confusion.

'Do forgive me, gentlemen,' she said. 'I did not intend to deceive you, but at the time of our meeting I was travelling incognito. I really had no idea that we would meet again so soon.'

For myself I could have forgiven that lovely creature anything. Even the hard-bitten O'Neill was charmed by her. 'It is of no consequence,' he said.

The evening was a great success. O'Neill and I were greatly charmed by the Gore-Booth family, whom, unlike so many of their aristocratic background, were warm, candid and totally at their ease with all members of society. The richest landowner and the poorest musician were both treated with the same respect and consideration.

Before very long, I had the pleasure of a talk with Captain Grey-Wynn, whom it transpired held more than a passing interest in the adventures of Sherlock Holmes.

The Reverend Le-Fanu introduced me to a local man who had recently made something of a name for himself in literary circles. 'It is always a pleasure to introduce men of letters to each other,' he said. 'Dr Watson meet Mr Douglas Hyde.'

'Dr Watson, your fame has spread even to this far corner of the world,' said Mr Hyde, cordially.

'I am honoured indeed,' I said, 'when an eminent writer such as yourself has bothered with my poor fare.'

It was a few moments later when I felt a tugging at my sleeve and a harsh whisper in my ear. It was O'Neill. He seemed much agitated. 'Watson, look at the figure standing on the top step, by the long windows.'

'Good heavens, it is Taffe.'

'How on earth did the man manage to get in?'

'I do not know. I think, however, that it would not be wise to make it known to him that he has been observed.'

'Indeed, he is certainly a dangerous customer.'

O'Neill and I slipped away from the throng. Under the cover of the bushes we were able to observe our man without any danger of ourselves being seen by him.

'Look,' I said. 'He is coming this way.'

'We must assail him.'

'Indeed. Quiet, he is coming.'

As the man passed the bushes, he must have been totally astounded to find himself grasped by two pairs of hands and thrown roughly to the ground.

'Now my beauty, we have got you,' I said.

'My dear fellow,' came a voice I instantly recognized. 'Is it totally necessary for you to be so melodramatic?'

'Holmes, is it you?'

There have been many occasions in my life when total surprise has overtaken me, but finding Sherlock Holmes at a party in Sligo, disguised as an opprobrious character, was certainly the greatest.

My discovery made me feel both foolish and angry.

Holmes had deceived me into thinking him to be on the Continent, when all the time he had been trailing O'Neill and myself across Ireland.

'Holmes, what is the meaning of this?'

'Doctor, if you please, do not shout. I have no wish to be exposed quite yet.'

'You must explain,' I said, hotly.

'Of course, but I beg you, Watson, this is neither the time nor the place. Let us enjoy the party for a little time, then we may make our excuses and leave. I will then explain myself to you.'

I helped Holmes to his feet. He brushed himself down and reset his wig. He was not a moment too soon. Captain Grey-Wynn appeared. 'There you are, we have missed you,' he said. 'Ah, I see you have met Mr Taffe.'

'Eh, oh yes,' I said.

'These gentlemen were just remarking on the lush vegetation to be found in Sligo,' said Holmes artlessly. 'We have just returned from a closer inspection of some of the more choice elements.'

'If you are truly interested in matters arboreal,' said the captain, 'then you must surely see the area surrounding my home at Hazelwood House.'

'Why, thank you, sir,' said Holmes.

'Now you really must come back to the lights. Willie Yeates is about to give us one of his poems. Yeates is a bit of a queer beggar, but he has a way with words.'

Back in the light, an olive-skinned man was standing rather self-consciously with a book in his hand. The music in the words was plain to hear as he spoke of Ireland's green fields and surprising people.

Holmes snorted, he had no time for culture. He and

King George I shared a common dislike of all 'boets and bainters'. 'It is all clap-trap and nonsense,' he said.

'Oh dear, Mr Taffe,' came a clear charming voice from our left. It was Constance Gore-Booth. 'Poetry is an art in which the Irish excel. When I go to Europe next year it will be a piquant reminder of what I leave behind.'

'Mr Taffe is very down to earth,' I said.

Holmes gave a light laugh. 'Tonight, Doctor, I have been even further down to earth than usual.'

The chimes of midnight had just faded away. From the rest of the great house there came hardly a sound. Holmes, O'Neill and myself were the only occupants not deep in slumber.

'Now, Holmes, will you explain the meaning of this charade,' I said.

'Certainly, Doctor,' he said. 'Some ten days ago, O'Neill arrived in London for his annual visit. At the behest of Sir George Moore, he accepted a small jet stick pin. This small object purports to be of far greater value than either Mr O'Neill or you, Doctor, can imagine. As a piece of jewellery it has no great intrinsic value, but as the last remaining piece of an ancient Celtic jewel set, it is priceless.'

'You are saying that I am carrying on my person a part of a set of jewels belonging to the ancient halls of Tara?'

Holmes smiled, 'No, O'Neill, you are not.'

'Then I fail to understand you,' said O'Neill.

'The stick pin you are carrying is a copy. Only there is someone who is convinced that it is the genuine jewel.'

'And this man is behind the attacks on O'Neill?' I said.

'Exactly.'

'You have made no attempt to prevent them?'

'On the contrary. O'Neill, do you remember the clerical gentleman who returned to you your wallet?'

'That was you?' said O'Neill.

'It was.'

'The man who helped apprehend the villain who caused O'Neill to need stitches, that was you as well?'

'Yes.'

'Mr Taffe who apprehended the thief in Dublin. Of course, it is all clear now,' said O'Neill. 'You were picking off the gang one by one.'

'Exactly. My intervention ensured the capture of his minions. He would be forced into an attempt in person.'

'The consequences of which almost cost a life,' I said.

Holmes gave a grim smile. 'I did not allow for him shooting at you. That was a serious miscalculation.'

'What will this man do now?' I said. 'Indeed, who is this man, Holmes?'

'His name is Petter Van Der Elst. He is the most accomplished criminal since the demise of Professor Moriarty.'

'You inform us that the jewel in the stick pin is worth a great deal of money,' said O'Neill. 'Who would be willing to pay such sums?'

'There are many who are very willing, Mr O'Neill,' said Holmes. 'Americans of Irish origin who desire a piece of their heritage, no matter how tiny. There are three European noblemen who are collectors of ancient jewellery and there is at least one English lord who is more than willing to expend several thousands of pounds on such an object.'

'You believe that Van Der Elst will make another attempt to steal the pin?' said O'Neill.

'Undoubtedly,' said Holmes.

'Only this time we will be ready for him,' I said.

'Exactly.'

'What is your plan, Holmes?' I said.

'Tomorrow morning when we part, you, O'Neill, will announce that you intend to visit Captain Grey-Wynn at Hazelwood House. I have no doubt that our man will be paying close attention to our conversation and it will be easy to convince him into following us.

'You, Watson, will allow O'Neill to get down on the west side of Lough Gill. You will then turn back to the road and wait in a secluded area which I will indicate to you as we proceed. I will ride off to the north of the house and wait in my predetermined hiding place.

'Now you, O'Neill, I expect you to have very little time to spare between getting down from the carriage and the moment when you are accosted. Here is a football referee whistle. You must blow it. We will be at your side within sixty seconds. Do you understand?'

O'Neill grew a little pale but spoke with a firm conviction. 'Yes, Mr Holmes, I understand.'

'Excellent,' said Holmes. 'Now let us to bed.'

The next morning I awoke to the sound of the rain lashing against my bedroom window. Holmes was not at all pleased with the change in the weather. 'It is possible that the weather will hinder our plans,' he said. 'Nevertheless, we must persist.'

Later in the morning we took our leave of the Gore-Booth family. Although Sir Josslyn was absent on estate duties, his mother and sister remained to bid us farewell. Lady Gore-Booth shook me by the hand. 'Goodbye, Dr Watson. I do so hope we shall meet again before you return to London.'

I shook hands with Miss Constance. 'Goodbye and thank you for your kindness.'

'Goodbye, Dr Watson. I expect we will meet again.'

Sherlock Holmes bowed low and shook the ladies' hands. O'Neill saluted and climbed aboard our trap.

'Not a pleasant day for travelling,' said Holmes. 'However, I have to be about my business and I know that O'Neill intends to visit your cousin, the captain, whatever the weather.'

The trap splashed along the wet roads. Holmes rode closely alongside. We had turned onto the Colagh Road when Holmes tapped my shoulder with his riding whip. 'Watson,' he said. 'Our man is in pursuit. He has taken the bait.'

The road turned towards Hazelwood House. Holmes pointed to a large copse of beech trees which formed a rough triangle. 'Now, Watson, when you have deposited O'Neill, you will drive back to this copse and await the sound of his whistle. I will ride ahead for a short way, then turn up that track you can see a hundred yards ahead where I, too, will pause until I hear O'Neill's whistle.'

I drove O'Neill a further hundred yards or so. He then alighted. I pressed my hand onto his shoulder. 'Good luck, old man,' I said. 'Do not wait for the villain to attack you before sounding the alarm.'

O'Neill smiled faintly. 'Do not concern yourself on that matter, John. I am not the stuff from which heroes are made.'

I turned around the trap and quickly whipped the horses into a gallop. Moments later I stood waiting in my hiding place.

There was the sound of a horse passing by. I had to stand

on the seat to see. A blond man was riding a bay. It was undoubtedly Van Der Elst. The Dutchman reined in his horse as he saw the figure of O'Neill. Then as quick as a flash he spurred on his horse again.

O'Neill had obviously heard the rider's approach because he spun around to face him. His hand came up to his mouth and I heard the shrill blast of the whistle.

Quickly, I whipped the horses into action. O'Neill was now running from his pursuer. He fell, slipping on the muddy ground. Van Der Elst was on him in an instant.

For a moment they struggled on the grass. O'Neill threw his man. Van Der Elst was quickly on his feet. Hearing my approach, he stopped.

There was a bang and a bullet sang past my head. I gritted my teeth and whipped the horses on. Then from the hill came a rider on a charge. It was Sherlock Holmes.

Van Der Elst, finally realizing that it was a trap, ran for his horse, but Holmes was upon him. Like an avenging angel, Holmes struck his man down. I reined in my horses and jumped down. Holmes had his man in a vice-like grip.

'Now, my beauty, I have you,' he said, grimly.

But Van Der Elst was not yet done. By hooking his leg about his captor's leg, he was able to overbalance Holmes. Swiftly he ran. It was not for the road, however, but for the lake.

'The pin,' cried O'Neill. 'He has the pin.'

Seconds later the pin was gently residing on the lake bottom. Van Der Elst gave a sneer. 'Now, Mr Sherlock Holmes, no one will have the treasure.'

O'Neill and I looked at each other quite aghast. Sherlock Holmes, however, threw back his head and laughed. 'The pin that you have taken endless trouble to steal and to then destroy is a fake. Nothing more, nothing less.'

'Of course it is,' I said. 'In the excitement I had quite forgotten.'

Van Der Elst looked at the three grinning faces in blank astonishment. 'A fake, Goot Gott!'

A damp Irish day was turning into a damp Irish night. Van Der Elst had been deposited into the cells of Sligo police station and Holmes, O'Neill and myself found ourselves once more under the roof of the Gore-Booth family at Lissadell.

Holmes sat languidly before the crackling woodfire. About him, like a court surrounding its monarch, sat Constance Gore-Booth, Douglas Hyde and the newly arrived Sir George Moore, Hugo O'Neill and myself.

'Holmes,' I said. 'Perhaps you can now explain the events and your part in them. All of us know part of the story but none of us know the whole.'

Sherlock Holmes smiled faintly, sat forward in his chair and laid his pipe on the stand beside him. 'When our friend, O'Neill, here arrived in London, Sir George presented him with a stick pin which purported to be part of a national treasure. Sir George had earlier discovered that this tiny piece of jet was from the treasures belonging to the Halls of Tara.

'It was unfortunate that the news of this great discovery had somehow been relayed to a certain Petter Van Der Elst, a criminal of European reputation. As a consequence, Sir George approached me and asked for my advice.

'There are many potential purchasers of such a treasure and I was convinced that Van Der Elst would be unable to resist any opportunity of stealing the pin if it came his way.

'Unfortunately my scheme entailed the involvement of a cat's paw. I had no doubt that Van Der Elst would be informed of the change of owner and that his minions would soon be set to work. For such a duplicity, O'Neill, I beg you to forgive me.

'I had to play a lone hand and a long game. One by one I whittled down the gang. You will remember, O'Neill, the two attempts in London? Van Der Elst lost two of his gang to the police courts.

'Once you arrived in Ireland, I had to adopt a new persona. I became Michael Taffe. Your feet hardly touched the streets of Dublin when I was able to round up another of his henchmen.

'At Longford, I was able to waylay the final member of his gang when he was arrested red-handed filching your luggage, Watson. For which I do apologize, Doctor, because in the excitement, it was left on the station. In fact, the train very nearly departed without me.

'At this point, Van Der Elst was on his own, but I reasoned that after coming so far he would not simply just give up. I was proved to be correct. Twice he made attempts to injure O'Neill.

'On the first occasion, a gunshot on Knocknarea sent a chip of granite spinning into his eye. Unfortunately, I was unable to follow Watson and O'Neill that day, as I had business elsewhere.

'It was at Glencar that I nearly had my man. Watson, you had surprised him and I only just allowed him to evade me. You will no doubt remember the incident.

'I decided that there was now nothing to be gained from remaining in the guise of Mr Taffe before Watson and O'Neill, because it was clear to me that their assistance was vital to the capture of Van Der Elst. And so it was to be so, the villain is now in charge and the treasure is safe.'

'Wonderful,' I cried. 'It is not a boast that many can make when they can tell their friends, I have saved a national treasure.'

'Even if I was duped into it,' said O'Neill, darkly.

'Surely, Hugo, you will not hold a grudge,' I said.

O'Neill looked carefully at Sherlock Holmes, relaxed and smiled. 'No, even though I nearly received a bullet in my back as a reward.'

O'Neill stood up and held out his hand, which Holmes took.

'But the real treasure,' I said. 'You say it is safe, Holmes?'

'Safe and in Ireland.'

'But how?'

Holmes smiled. 'Step forward, Miss Noel.'

Constance Gore-Booth smiled and from beneath the frill of her collar, produced an identical stick pin. 'Here, Mr Holmes.'

Holmes smiled. 'Thank you, Miss Gore-Booth, but do not give it to me, give it to Mr Hyde.'

Douglas Hyde took the stick pin and held it up to the light.

'Wonderful,' he said. 'One of Ireland's treasures has come home at last.'

The train journey from Carrick on Shannon to Dublin had been uneventful, as most railway journeys are. Sherlock Holmes was looking languidly at the scenery. 'This has been a holiday to remember, eh, Doctor?' he said.

'It has certainly been an experience I shall never forget. It is one that O'Neill will never forget either.'

'Yes, I am truly repentant for placing you both in such danger and not informing you of the chances you were taking.'

'As you should be,' I said. 'However, I do perceive that if O'Neill and I had been put on our guard, we should not have acted so naturally.'

'Exactly, you would have put Van Der Elst on his guard and I could never have laid and caught our man in such a simple trap.'

The train slowed as it came into the station. Holmes pulled down the hand luggage. 'You will have another holiday this year, Watson?'

'I expect so,' I said.

'What of your destination?'

I laughed. 'If ever I take another holiday, it will not be in Ireland, it will not be with O'Neill and it will certainly not involve Sherlock Holmes. I believe I shall spend the entire time securely locked up in my bedroom!'

The Strange Affair at Glastonbury

It was a cold October morning when I came down to breakfast at 221B Baker Street, to find Sherlock Holmes had decided to indulge in a little spring-cleaning. The fact that it was not spring, and that his undertaking did not result in any cleaning, seemed hardly to matter to him; for when I returned from my afternoon rounds to the rooms we shared, I found him sitting cross-legged on the floor, surrounded by a perfect sea of newsprint, papers and note-books.

I hung up my overcoat and threw my bag onto the table. 'Good heavens, Holmes. The whole place is in uproar, worse than when I departed this morning.'

Holmes looked up at me and smiled briefly. 'It is not unusual, Watson. Before any sense of order may be achieved, a greater disorder than existed originally must ensue.'

Picking my way through the debris, I reached my arm-chair and sat warming my hands and feet before the fire. Holmes, of course, was exactly right. In order to success-fully re-arrange any collection, it is necessary to have it spread out before one.

Reaching down, I selected from a pile one of the old notebooks into which I had written up some of our adven-tures. As I casually thumbed through the pages, I smiled. Fond memories of events, both weighty and trivial, came back to mind. Here was my first account of the 'Adventure of the Copper Beeches', followed by 'The Greek Interpreter' and 'The Red-Headed League.'

It was as I turned to the next case, one I have yet to judge suitable for publication, that some carefully-folded foolscap sheets fell out onto my lap. Puzzled, I laid down the notebook upon the side table and examined the papers.

'My word!' I exclaimed.

Holmes looked up from his activities. 'What is it, Watson?'

'It is a report on our Glastonbury adventure. I have to admit that I had quite forgotten all about it . . . until now.'

Holmes jumped to his feet and came to look over my shoulder. He laughed. 'Ha! So that is to where it had disappeared. Tell me, my dear fellow. How did it come to be tucked into a notebook recording our adventures in 1890?'

I pulled a face. 'I really cannot remember,' I said. 'I do recall, however, that when I wrote these notes I was concerned that the events could be somewhat sensitive and had decided to let the matter rest for a year or so before bringing it to the public's attention.'

Holmes looked at me through heavily-lidded eyes. 'If memory serves, Watson, these events took place some five years ago. What possessed you to insert these notes into a collection of cases which took place some five years earlier, and then to forget all about them?'

I sighed, this was Holmes at his most irritating.

'I seem to recall that when I was writing up the notes, it occurred to me that the case bore some similarities to one you had solved in that year. Perhaps I was referring to them when a new and more urgent case was brought to my attention and I placed these sheets in the notebook for safe keeping and later recovery.'

'Then you forgot about them completely,' he said. 'It was very remiss of you, Doctor.'

A trifle nettled by his tone, I took the argument to Sherlock Holmes. 'It seems to me, Holmes, had you taken better care of your archives and indexed them more carefully, then my oversight would not have taken so long to come to light.'

Holmes snorted, but he was prevented from replying to my barb by the timely arrival of Mrs Hudson. The good lady surveyed the scene with undisguised horror. 'Mr Holmes! Dr Watson! I had intended to discuss supper. I have a game pie in the kitchen, but I see now that this house is better suited to bread and cheese.'

Alarmed at the prospect of a delicious dinner disappearing into the ether, so to speak, I immediately jumped to my feet and began tidying away some of the debris. Mrs Hudson said nothing more, but departed secure in the knowledge that her warning had not gone unheeded.

'Take care not to mislay those papers again, Watson,' said Holmes slyly as he sat at the table idly surveying my hurried attempts to organize the room. 'If, after supper, we desire to review that case, it would not do if we could not find them again.'

Good fortune, allied to the kindly and forgiving nature of our landlady, decreed that our meal was not bread and cheese. An hour later, therefore, Holmes and I sat before a roaring fire drinking our brandies and soda and discussing the nature of our newly re-discovered case.

After much deliberation, therefore, I now set down, in as much detail as possible after all these years, the singular events that led me to entitle this adventure, 'The Strange Affair at Glastonbury.'

It was during the final weeks of 1895 when Sherlock Holmes received an urgent communication from the diocese of Bath and Wells, concerning a prominent church official who had found himself embroiled in a financial matter of particular sensitivity. Holmes had immediately replied by telegram that he proposed to take the first available train from Paddington and would be in Bath that very afternoon.

'You will travel with me, Watson?' he said. 'I would greatly value your company and support, for I fear that this case may be a protracted affair.'

'If you will have me,' I replied, 'I would be delighted. My practice is closed for the season and there will be very little to occupy me for some time.'

'Excellent,' he said. 'Then it is settled.'

The affair, a delicate and somewhat tangled matter, was concluded with a speed which surprised even Sherlock Holmes. We were left, therefore, with time on our hands. Holmes, as a consequence, considered telegraphing Mrs Hudson, warning her that we were returning somewhat earlier than expected.

Holmes was about to scribble a note for the boy to dispatch to London, when I laid my hand upon his arm. 'I wonder, my dear fellow,' I said tentatively. 'As time appears to be very much in our favour, would it be possible for us to visit a town I have often wished to see?'

He laid down his pen and gazed at me. 'Tomorrow we travel to Wells to pay a visit on His Grace the Bishop. Afterwards the world is our oyster. So why not, Watson, why not?' he smiled that sharp smile. 'Whither do we travel, old fellow?'

'Not far. It is to Glastonbury. Oh, I know that you will

not approve, but it is a place of legend and mystery, and ever since I was a boy it has been a magnet to me. Never before have I been so close and the pull is so very strong now.'

'Spoken like the poet you are, my boy,' said Holmes. He slapped me on the shoulder. 'We shall travel to Glastonbury as soon as the Bishop is done with us.'

It was three-thirty the next afternoon and Sherlock Holmes and I were waiting on Wells Station, anticipating the train that would convey us to Glastonbury. We had enjoyed a convivial lunch with His Grace and had witnessed an attraction unique to the city. It was the sight of swans on the moat surrounding the Bishop's Palace, ringing a small bell placed under one of the windows by reaching up to a string and pulling at it with their beaks. Their reward was to be fed by one of the palace officials. I wondered at the time, what would Mr Darwin make of it?

Then, with a roar and hiss, our conveyance arrived. A weak winter sun shone down upon the red and brown carriages of the Somerset and Dorset train as we stepped aboard.

'Glastonbury next stop,' declared the porter as he helped Holmes and myself with our bags. 'Takes about fifteen minutes,' he further volunteered. 'You'll be met by a driver from the George in the High Street.'

I thanked this veritable mine of information and pulled up the window. Then we were off. At last I was to visit the town of my boyhood dreams.

True to expectation, a carriage from the hotel was waiting for the train. As we walked through the concourse and into the road, the driver jumped down and touched his hat with his whip. 'Good afternoon, gentlemen. We'll have you in town in just five minutes,' he cried as he took our bags and quickly piled them up by his seat.

Before very long we were rattling along the quiet narrow lanes, the bare trees and hedges framing the road ahead. Very soon we were driving up the road into the town.

'This is Benedict Street,' said our driver, waving his whip at the lines of red-bricked houses. 'There's a few shops along here past the church, but the main shopping is done at Magdalene Street at the top and the High Street up the hill beyond.'

The carriage swung into Magdalene Street and past the town cross. Our hotel was near by on the left at the foot of the High Street. Holmes had telegraphed ahead. Two bedrooms and a private sitting room had been procured for a week.

A little later, after I had unpacked, I wandered into our sitting room. Holmes was sitting before the fire reading a copy of *The Avalon Independent*, Glastonbury's own newspaper. He looked up from the gossip column. 'Are your plans for the next few days to include a walk up the famous Glastonbury Tor, Watson?'

I sat in the armchair and warmed myself before the fire. 'Indeed,' I replied. 'Tomorrow, weather permitting.' I took out of my jacket pocket a local guidebook, thoughtfully supplied by the hotel. 'It says here that on a clear day it is possible to see four counties.'

Holmes cast an eye towards the window where the grey afternoon light was accompanied by a slight drizzle, the spots of rain being forced against the glass by a fresh breeze. I sighed. 'Then again, perhaps not,' I continued.

'The perils of holidaying in the English winter,' he remarked, smiling briefly.

After supper the hotel proprietor, Mr Poole, came into our sitting room. He appeared slightly uneasy in his manner and after a stilted conversation, he came to the matter that had clearly been bothering him. 'I hope you will excuse my forwardness, gentlemen, but you are Mr Sherlock Holmes and Dr Watson, the celebrated detectives?'

I cast a quick glance at Holmes before replying. 'We are indeed, sir. Although in all conscience I cannot remotely describe myself as a detective.'

'Will you not convey to us what it is that is bothering you, Mr Poole?' said Holmes sharply.

Our host pulled up a hard-backed chair and sat between Holmes and myself before the fire. 'It is a small and somewhat insignificant matter, but I believe it will arrest your attention, Mr Holmes.'

Holmes nodded. 'Then please continue, sir.'

'Early this morning it was discovered that during the night every signpost in the town had been turned to face the wrong direction. I can tell you, sir, that it caused a fine old fuss, particularly from those unfamiliar with the roads around here.'

'Could they have been changed by youngsters playing a prank?' I asked.

'Well, I suppose it's possible, Dr Watson, but it was a job and a half and I don't believe that kids would've bothered with it, particularly as none of 'em were around to observe the consequences.'

'Indeed?'

'Yes, there was the driver for Clark Brothers Shoe Factory in Street; he was new to the job and instead of taking the Street Road, he ended up stuck on Northload Bridge with a broken axle and quite unable to turn the cart around.

I suppose it was a good job that the farm was just up the way, for the farmhands and Mr James, the shopkeeper, at least got it out of the road.'

Mr Poole stood up and smiled. 'It might seem a trivial incident to you, Mr Holmes, but it cost a lot of people time and money. Let's hope that's the last of it, eh?'

'Thank you, Mr Poole,' said Holmes. 'That was most interesting.'

Morning had broken over Somerset. It was the birth of a new day, but the weather had not improved, for from my bed I could hear the sound of rain against the window. Clearly any outdoor activities would have to be postponed.

The next few hours passed slowly. After breakfast I perused the newspapers, then I conversed with Holmes on the matter of criminality, and finally I stood watching the local populace tramping the wet and shiny streets of the town. I looked at my watch, it was nearly twelve and my mind began to turn to thoughts of luncheon.

Suddenly, Mr Poole appeared in the doorway. 'Mr Holmes, Dr Watson. You will never guess what has occurred?'

'My dear sir,' said Holmes, solemnly, 'I never guess, it is a shocking habit which wastes time and is not conducive to deduction.'

'What has happened, Mr Poole?' I enquired of the flustered hotelier.

'It's like this, sir. This morning it was discovered that the blooms on the Glastonbury thorn had all been cut off overnight.'

'Blooms?' I said. 'You have a shrub which flowers in December?'

'Indeed. The Glastonbury thorn is a well-known variety, which has flowered every winter for as long as anyone can remember. People around here regard it as a national treasure. Why, sprigs of the thorn are annually cut off and sent to Her Majesty as a token of our felicity.' Mr Poole frowned. 'This is more than a silly prank, like the other; the town is up in arms about it.'

Holmes said nothing; he merely stood up and reached for his coat and hat. Then for the longest moment he stood, head bowed in thought. 'Where can this remarkable plant be found, Mr Poole?' he said at last.

'It is in front of the church of St John the Baptist up the High Street.'

'Indeed,' I said. 'That will explain the large number of people I have observed milling about today.'

The church of St John was to be found towards the middle of the High Street. Before its fine perpendicular frontage stood the thorn, a small gnarled tree reaching twisted fingers into the cold, grey, winter sky.

Despite the rain and the general chill of the day, a large number of townspeople were gathered around discussing the matter in low tones.

Holmes sighed. 'It is as I feared, Watson. Any evidence has long been all but obliterated by the countless numbers of casual onlookers. It is a pity that the police did not place a *cordon sanitaire* around the area when the misdeed was discovered.'

'You speak as if you are familiar with the work of the detective, sir,' said a rich, fruity voice from behind Holmes and myself. Turning quickly, I discovered our interlocutor to be none other than a policeman. He saluted respectfully. 'Sergeant Buckland, at your service, gentlemen.'

'You are correct, Sergeant,' said Holmes. 'I am familiar with the arts of detection. Permit me to introduce myself and my companion. I am Sherlock Holmes and this is Dr John Watson.'

A broad smile spread across the policeman's face. 'Then it is true. Old Poole of the George said you was in town.' He thrust out his hand in a gesture of welcome. 'It is an honour to meet you both.'

It was fortunate that the crowd had thinned out somewhat and Sergeant Buckland was able to show us the little he had gleaned from his own investigation.

He led Holmes and myself over to the tree. 'Now, sir. If you would care to inspect the earth around the thorn, you will see several places where the feet of a ladder have stood. If you look carefully you'll see that the earth is quite hard but the ladder has still been pushed quite a long way into it. I would imagine that the miscreant is quite heavy. More than twelve stones.'

'Excellent,' cried Holmes.

'There's more, sir,' said the policeman. 'On the bark of the tree, I found this.' He opened his tunic and took out a folded envelope. He passed it to Holmes.

Holmes opened the envelope and tipped something into his hand. 'It is a swirl of wood,' he said. 'What do you make of it, Watson? It is singular, is it not?'

He held it up for my inspection. 'It is certainly quite unusual,' I agreed. 'I have never seen what appears to be new wood in a spiral shape before. Perhaps it is the dross from woodworking.'

'It has clearly been cut from a much larger piece,' said Holmes. 'Have you noticed any more under foot, Sergeant?'

The policeman shook his head. 'No, Sir, too many feet had preceded me.'

'Ah well. Never mind, you have done well, nevertheless.'

'Thank you, Mr Holmes.'

The sergeant cleared his throat and looked pensive. 'Excuse me, Mr Holmes, Dr Watson. Perhaps, one evening you would care to join the wife and me for an early supper? She has read all your books, Dr Watson, and I think it would be a great honour for her, indeed for me, if you gentlemen would care to join us at our table, say . . . Wednesday?'

Holmes and I glanced at each other.

'My dear Sergeant Buckland,' I said. 'We should regard it as a signal honour. How does six-thirty suit you?'

The next morning I awoke to discover the sun shining in a blue sky. The rain of the previous day had gone and it seemed as if the fates had finally conspired to assist us. No doubt the slopes of the Glastonbury Tor would be wet and slippery, but I was determined not to be put off by some mud.

Holmes greeted me at the table. He had finished his egg and was by now consuming a quantity of hot, strong coffee.

'Good morning, Doctor. I see that the weather has relented. My hiking boots are entirely at your disposal.'

It was a little after ten am when Holmes and myself stepped out once more onto the streets of Glastonbury. We had gone no more than a few paces, however, when we were overtaken by Sergeant Buckland. 'Good morning, gentlemen,' he said. 'I do not know if we have yet another prank or whatever you might call it, but I've just had Appleby's boy at the station telling me that the governor's having a fit over his stolen sign.'

'Indeed,' said Holmes. 'If you do not mind, Sergeant, we shall join you in your enterprise.'

Appleby's proved to be one of the town's butchers or 'High-class Purveyors of Meat' as the signwriter would have it. Mr Appleby was at the door. His large red face was contorted with anger. 'There you are at last, Buckland,' he cried at the policeman. 'What are you going to do about my stolen sign?'

The sergeant took out his notebook and began to write. 'Well now, Mr Appleby, let's get a few facts down on paper to start with. This sign, can you describe it for me?'

The butcher almost jumped into the air with vexation. 'Describe it?' he cried. 'You know what it looks like, you've seen it often enough.' He sighed, realizing that a process had to be gone into, said resignedly, 'It's about five feet high, ox-shaped, made of cast iron and painted.'

'Thank you, sir,' said the sergeant affably. 'Now, when did you last see it?'

'Last night, when we closed up shop. About seven-thirty it was. I left it in its usual place outside the shop. Someone must have pinched it during the night.'

'Excuse me, sir,' interrupted Holmes. 'Why do you not take it in at night?'

'You deaf?' said the butcher. 'I said it's made of cast iron. It's much too heavy to keep moving about. I can tell you, mister, when old Churchill, the blacksmith, delivered it he had two of his lads to help him. I'm a strong man, but I have trouble shifting it. So it stays outside.'

Sherlock Holmes nodded. Then quite suddenly and much to the surprise of Mr Appleby and the sergeant, he dropped to his knees and examined the ground in front of the butcher's shop. 'Look at this, Watson. The sign was dragged to the kerb, see the scoring of the flags? It was half-dragged, half-walked to a low-bodied conveyance.' He moved over to the gutter. 'Ah, look. A not inconsiderable amount of debris, which doubtless fell off the underside of the vehicle when the sign was deposited upon it.'

Sergeant Buckland stooped down and picked up some of the debris. It appeared to be mud. He smiled. 'Well,' he said, thoughtfully, 'perhaps it will prove to be relevant.'

'Excellent, Sergeant,' cried Holmes. 'Earth has many differences. Perhaps an investigation will locate it to a particular part of town.'

He brushed the dust of the street off his knees. 'I do not think that we need to tarry any longer. We shall see you again tomorrow, then perhaps you may have something for us.'

Sherlock Holmes and I continued our walk up the High Street, then turned right along Lansdown Street and into Chilkwell Street. Then before us we espied a large and ancient tithe barn.

'The property of the church, or I am no judge,' said Holmes.

Then, we were on the grassy lower slopes of the Tor. As I climbed the steep incline, my legs grew progressively more tired, but when at last we crested the brow and stood beside the ruin of St Michael's Church, all feelings of fatigue were swept away. Below, like some gigantic patchwork quilt, lay Somerset. Mile upon mile of flat tree-lined land, with small clusters of farms and hamlets tucked into the lee of the trees met our gaze. Rivers and ancient drainage culverts glinted in the sun, running like ribbons, they cut the sward into many shapes and sizes. Looking to the south, I could see the smoking factory chimneys of Bridgwater, and beyond there was the sudden rise to the Quantock Hills. To the west was another hill, quite alone, called Brent Knoll, and to the north another range of hills, reaching to the waters of the Bristol Channel, the Mendips.

I took off my cap and wiped the perspiration away with my handkerchief. The breeze tugged at my hair and pecked at my trouser legs. I took a deep breath. 'Wonderful,' I remarked.

I gazed idly down on the road between Glastonbury and Street, the two towns almost reaching out to touch each other. Street, the shoe-making town with the factory of Clark Brothers and the rows of purpose-built houses.

Sherlock Holmes, however, had other matters to occupy his mind. 'There is a definite pattern emerging, Watson.'

'My dear fellow,' I remonstrated. 'Can we not put all thoughts of these occurrences out of our minds for just a little while? I cannot see any great national or international ramifications here, just a number of unrelated and rather silly events. Indeed, if this was a university town, I would expect some students to be responsible.'

Holmes gazed steadily at me. 'Ah, Watson, but these silly events, as you so eloquently describe them, do seem to fit into a pattern.'

'Oh indeed?' I replied. 'What possible pattern could there be?'

'Well, for one thing they must have kept the perpetrators busy for some considerable time,' he chuckled. 'Turning the signposts around must have taken them all night. I cannot envisage the removal and hiding of a large and heavy sign to have been executed in just a few minutes. As for the clipping of hundreds of blooms from the Glastonbury thorn, it had to take them at least two hours.' He poked me in the ribs with his pipe. 'And, my boy, where are the blooms? There were none to be seen in the churchyard.'

I shook my head. 'Well, that makes these nonsensical events even more bizarre. Why on earth should anyone in their right mind wish to commit such crimes and take so long over them? What possible purpose do they fulfil?'

'What purpose, indeed?' Holmes agreed, thoughtfully. 'However, my dear fellow,' he said suddenly. 'I believe that you are right. It is not a matter upon which we should ponder now, for it is, as you say, a day for other, less cerebral, activities. Let us, therefore, make our way back down into the town and seek out luncheon. Earlier, I noticed a capital establishment called Barratt Brothers in the High Street. So come along, Watson. No time to waste.'

I smiled to myself. How easily had I been inveigled by Holmes into a discussion about the recent events in the town. As I watched his rapidly disappearing form, I knew in my heart that, once again, Holmes had got the better of me. I also knew that he had got the bit between his teeth, and whatever else occurred he would see the matter through.

Luncheon was taken at the appointed establishment and it proved to be a pleasant if uneventful occasion. Indeed, the only moment of excitement came about when Holmes accidentally bumped into a portly, middle-aged and rather dusty-looking man, dressed in a black frock coat and grey trousers. He had been walking slowly, fishing around in his inside pockets, apparently quite oblivious to the world about him. The coming together with Sherlock Holmes, however, rudely brought him back to reality. A variety of papers and odds and ends became dislodged from his person and fell, scattered to the four winds. The man gazed dazedly about himself.

'I am so sorry, sir,' said Holmes, politely apologizing, when it was clearly not his fault. 'Here, let me assist you.'

Together Holmes, the man and I collected up the papers and objects. Then, with his property safely stored away, we sent him on his journey once more.

'What a strange and disjointed sort of fellow,' I remarked.

'A solicitor's clerk,' said Holmes, firmly.

'Really, Holmes. How can you possibly tell?'

Holmes looked sharply at me, but before he could answer, the man disappeared into the premises of Bulleid and Nixon, Solicitors and Commissioners for Oaths. 'Ha!' cried Holmes, in a triumphant voice. 'You see, Watson. A solicitor's office.'

'But the fellow could be visiting on business of his own,' I objected.

Holmes sighed. 'Really, Watson. By now you should be able to notice these little signs for yourself. Did you not observe the state of his right sleeve? It was shiny for several inches. His left elbow was also smooth. These are sure signs of the wearer spending a considerable part of his day writing — QED a clerk. His mode of dress would lead one to the conclusion that he is employed by a solicitor. Also, my boy, you failed to notice that one of the papers dropped by our friend was tied up with pink ribbon. I do not know of any other profession which employs this method. What else do you require?'

I sighed. 'I require nothing else.'

Then Holmes took pity on me. 'Never mind, old fellow. When it comes to writing, I could never ever approach your literary expertise, even if you do regularly err on the side of embellishment.'

With Holmes, even an apology was delivered with a sting in the tail!

The next morning I was rudely awoken by a heavy knock at my bedroom door. It was Mr Poole, the hotelier. 'I am sorry to wake you, Dr Watson, but the miscreant has struck again.'

'Where is Mr Holmes?' I asked, as I attempted to collect my thoughts.

'He is dressing and will be here shortly. In the meantime, I will have your breakfast served directly.'

Dressing as quickly as possible, I suddenly realized that I did not know exactly why I had been so rudely disturbed. At breakfast, however, I quickly discovered the reason.

Mr Poole, himself, served us. All the while he regaled Holmes and myself with the story of the missing flag of St George. 'It's like this, gentlemen,' he said as he cleared away the debris of our meal and sent the maid about her business. 'When McCloud, my head butler, made his way up to the balcony to fly the flag this morning, he discovered that some time overnight it had been taken from the cupboard where it is stored when not flying. What do you make of it, Mr Holmes?'

Sherlock Holmes gazed thoughtfully at our host for a few moments. Then he jumped to his feet. 'I believe that we should inspect the locality from where your flag was taken.'

Mr Poole smiled and nodded. 'I should be delighted to show you, Mr Holmes. If you will follow me, I shall lead the way.'

The balcony from where the flag of St George was flown was reached by a flight of dark, steep and narrow stairs. Mr Poole carried a lamp, which cast giant shadows upon the walls and ceiling. At the top of the flight, there stood a small door, no more than four feet in height. He produced a shiny silver key and proceeded to unlock a large padlock.

'It is a pity,' our host remarked. 'Until today we did not regard it as necessary to lock this door.'

'At what o'clock was this theft discovered?' I asked.

'It was at six am sharp when McCloud informed me about the theft. I immediately sent for our local carpenter and by seven the door was secured.'

'Then before the theft, anyone could have come up here?' I asked.

'Oh, indeed. We never before regarded the flag as something worth stealing.'

Holmes took Mr Poole by the elbow. 'Tell me, sir. How many people have had access to this area since the theft was detected?'

The hotelier thought for a moment. 'Only myself, McCloud and, of course, the carpenter.'

'Very good. Perhaps you will allow me to examine the area alone. Possibly there may still be clues to the identity of the culprit.'

Mr Poole stood aside, whilst Holmes squeezed past him and through the open door, through which the grey light of day was flooding. The hotelier gazed at me with raised eyebrows. He was clearly taken aback by the sharpness of Holmes's tone.

'Mr Holmes is a particular man,' I told him. 'And whilst his methods are unconventional, they invariably prove to be successful.'

As if to prove the point, there came a sharp cry of

triumph from the balcony. 'Ha! Watson, look at this.'

I followed Holmes up the steps and thrust my head and shoulders through the doorway.

'What is it, old fellow? What have you discovered?'

He held up what appeared to be a notebook, bound in morocco. 'Stand back, Watson. I am coming down,' he said. 'It is raining and this is a find that needs to be carefully inspected and I do not propose to become soaking wet so doing.'

It was a few minutes later, therefore, before Holmes was able to fully examine his find. In the meantime, the hotel proprietor had been dispatched with instructions to discover if the notebook was the property of a member of the hotel staff.

Holmes held out his find. 'Here you are, Watson. Tell me, what do you make of it?'

I took the rather bedraggled object and inspected it closely. 'I can immediately tell that it has been dropped in some mud . . . Let me see . . . Good heavens, Holmes, have you seen the contents?'

I returned the notebook. Holmes smiled. 'They are singular, are they not?'

'They appear to be pure gibberish.'

'Perhaps,' he said, enigmatically. 'Then perhaps not.' He thumbed the pages. 'Fascinating.'

Taking a sheet of foolscap from the bureau, Holmes copied out the four pages, which had been written upon:

E.H.L.	Sun	Plane of	Salvation we
	Moon	Enlightenment	who are of the
THE SONS	Tura		body hold power
	Woden	1st circle	over all.
OF 'H'	Thor		
	Frier	2nd circle	⊠
	Saturn		
		3rd circle	This is the sign
	N.B.		that binds us.
	Memorize		
		Neophyte =	
		E.H.L.	

I gazed upon the jumble of words and lists and thought for a moment. 'This seems to be redolent of witchcraft,' I remarked.

Holmes nodded. 'Indeed. That is a distinct possibility.'

'But surely, witchcraft died out in this country a hundred years or more ago?'

Holmes shook his head. 'Not so, Watson. I recall that a case came to court not more than two years ago, when a man from Worcestershire claimed that his wife was using witchcraft to disaffect him from her, so she could be rid of him.'

'Remarkable.'

'However, I do not believe that we are involved in the occult; it is something quite different.'

He picked up the paper and folded it up.

'You have some idea in mind?' I asked.

'Possibly, Doctor,' he said enigmatically. 'Possibly.'

It was a little before the appointed hour of our supper engagement with Sergeant Buckland and his wife, when the policeman solved the mystery of the ownership of the notebook. There was a knock at our sitting room door. To my surprise, it was none other than the sergeant standing there.

'Why, Sergeant Buckland. What brings you here? I suppose that you did not think that Holmes and myself would be in need of an escort?'

The policeman laughed. 'Not at all, sir, but it occurred to me that you might be in a position to help solve another little mystery for me.'

I smiled. 'Perhaps it is Holmes rather than myself you should be asking.'

'Not at all, Dr Watson. I believe that you may be just the man for me. Earlier today one of our townspeople, a Mr Lockyear, came to see me. Apparently he has mislaid a notebook and he thinks that it was lost when he was returning to Bulleid and Nixon, his place of employment, yesterday luncheon time. He bumped into a gentleman who was walking with a friend and the accident caused him to drop a number of legal papers he was carrying. Mr Lockyear described the two gentlemen as clearly persons of good breeding, as he put it, and strangers to the town. I have to say that he described Mr Holmes to a T. I wonder, Dr Watson, did you recall such an incident yesterday?'

'It was Holmes and myself,' I agreed. 'But I do not recall observing any notebook . . . except . . .'

Here, I was rudely interrupted by Holmes. 'I have the notebook, Sergeant,' he said. 'I had intended to surrender it tonight in the hope that the owner could be discovered.' He reached into his jacket pocket and produced the object of the policeman's desire.

Sergeant Buckland smiled. 'Mr Lockyear will be greatly relieved. I believe it contains some confidential material relating to his employment.'

Holmes shot an expressive glance in my direction. 'That

will no doubt explain the unusual language in which it is written,' he said evenly.

Sergeant Buckland looked at his watch. 'Well, if we are to return the notebook to its owner before supper, then we had better hurry.'

It was fortunate that Mr Lockyear resided in Benedict Street, his house being a mere thirty paces from the police station. The property, however, was a rather ramshackle affair. Not unlike its owner, I mused. It was built in three storeys and had a slate roof with many damaged or missing slates and was in need of painting.

The front door was opened by a young man in workman's overalls. His dark, handsome face bore a scowl, but when he recognized the sergeant, his expression was transformed into a welcoming smile.

'Sergeant Buckland,' he said in a well-educated voice. 'How nice to see you again. Have you found Mr Lockyear's notebook?'

'Good evening, Mr Beck. That is why I have called. These gentlemen have found it and are keen to see it once again in the hands of its rightful owner.'

The young man ushered the sergeant, Holmes and myself into the front parlour, where a good fire was going. He gestured for us to sit down, then rushed off to find Mr Lockyear. As he opened the door to the kitchen, the noise of machinery, evident since the opening of the front door, became considerably louder. A few moments later, however, the noise ceased and the man with whom Holmes had been in collision appeared. On this occasion he was dressed in workman's trousers and shirtsleeves.

'Good evening, Sergeant. Young Beck tells me that you have recovered my notebook.' He peered somewhat myopically at Holmes and myself. 'Goodness me. These are the very gentlemen into whom I ran yesterday luncheon time.'

Holmes stepped forward and made the introductions. 'I am Sherlock Holmes and this is my friend and colleague, Dr Watson.'

'Glad to know you, gentlemen, and thank you. Will you not stay and have some tea with us?'

'No, thank you, Mr Lockyear, Mrs Buckland is awaiting us for supper,' said Holmes. 'We do not wish to keep the good lady waiting, neither do we desire to keep you from your carpentry.'

The solicitor's clerk stiffened visibly. 'Carpentry, how could you possibly know that I have been engaged in carpentry, Mr Holmes?'

Sherlock Holmes reached forwards and pulled a small swirl of wood from the turned-back cuff of Mr Lockyear's shirt and held it up. He smiled his quick smile. 'Elementary, my dear sir. I have also noted the telltale deposit of sawdust on your right slipper and some chips of wood in your hair. I would say, Mr Lockyear, that you have been sawing, turning and planing this evening.'

Sergeant Buckland laughed. 'My dear Mr Holmes, your reputation is not undeserved. Dear me, Mr Lockyear, I hope you never do anything underhand, for Mr Holmes will surely find you out.'

Our host smiled, but he did not look amused, however. He merely ushered us out onto the street. 'Thank you, gentlemen,' he said. 'Good night.'

Sergeant Buckland briefly deserted us to look in on the police station and I took the opportunity to quiz Holmes about the notebook.

'Why did you not choose to reveal exactly how the notebook came into your possession?'

Holmes, quite as usual, was enigmatic in his reply. 'I have my reasons, Doctor,' he said. 'But let me ask you a question. Did you not find our meeting with the household of Mr Lockyear to be illuminating?'

'We have discovered that the man enjoys woodworking in his spare time, but so do many others and they do not keep notebooks full of indecipherable writings.'

Holmes looked sharply at me. 'No, Watson. Consider instead the fact that there is considerably more than woodworking going on behind that front door.'

'Good heavens, Holmes. What do you mean?'

'I suppose that you did not notice the soiling of Mr Beck's overalls?'

I gave the matter a little thought. 'Certainly they were quite filthy. I assume that is what you are referring to . . .? They were stained with earth,' I cried in a triumphal tone. 'He has been digging the garden today.'

Holmes shook his head. 'Not quite right, Doctor. Old soil dries to a slate grey. The stains on his clothes were dark and quite fresh. No, he has been digging tonight.'

'But, what kind of man digs his garden in the dark?' I objected.

'What kind of man, indeed,' said Holmes quietly. 'We do seem to have a house of mysteries, do we not, Watson?'

The following morning Holmes and I were breakfasting when the boy brought in a telegram addressed to my friend. He slit open the envelope and quickly read the contents.

'It is from Lestrade. He wishes to consult me on a matter of the highest importance. Hmmm . . . He says that he is bringing a gentleman of some stature to see me on Saturday morning. Well, Watson, another case when this one remains uncompleted.'

'It is certainly awkward,' I said.

'Then we must solve this mystery in double-quick time,' he said firmly.

'Perhaps the catalogue of crimes has been ended,' I said hopefully.

Mr Poole, however, was soon at our table with news of yet another strange incident. 'It's the horse trough this time. Someone has emptied it during the night and they have left a tin cup tied by ribbon to one of the iron railings, presumably as a sign that it was with this mug that the water was removed.'

'Another of the labours of Hercules,' I mused.

'What was that, Watson?' said Holmes, sharply.

'I was merely remarking that these misdeeds seem to have taken on a Herculean aspect. Each of them must have taken considerable time and effort. They are rather like the tasks set by Eurystheus for Hercules to perform.'

Holmes jumped to his feet and much to my surprise and greatly to the consternation of our host, did a little jig of merriment. 'Watson,' he cried. 'I have said this before, but I believe it to be worth repeating. Whilst you yourself do not radiate light, you oft cause light to be shed where it is needed.'

'Thank you, Holmes,' I said. 'I do not pretend to remotely understand what it is that I have done to warrant your praise, but thank you just the same.'

Holmes took down his coat and hat from the peg and rubbed his hands together. 'No time for idle chatter, my boy. We must view this particular labour for ourselves.'

Sergeant Buckland was standing by the horse trough, surveying the empty vessel. He looked up at our approach and scowled. 'This really is the limit,' he said. 'Taking the water from the horses, and look,' he held up a tin mug, no bigger than a tea cup for our inspection, 'if they did indeed use this, then it must have taken them most of the night.'

Several other townsfolk were standing around, regarding the empty horse trough. One elderly man ventured an opinion. 'It is really too bad,' he said. 'Sergeant Buckland, our town has fallen victim to the most absurd practical joker. You simply have to take firm action.'

The others in the crowd murmured their assent. But it was the sudden movement of Sherlock Holmes which caught my eye. He had grasped at some ribbon still adhering to the railings and deposited it into his coat pocket.

'Come, Watson,' he said. 'There is nothing more to be done here.' He saluted Sergeant Buckland and disappeared in the direction of the hotel. I caught up with my friend as he passed over the threshold.

'It is exactly as I thought,' he said. 'A definite pattern has emerged. There is much more to this matter than meets the eye.'

'What do you mean, Holmes?'

'Simply this, Watson. These crimes are not an end in themselves, merely a means to an end.'

'Indeed?'

'It is a matter into which I need to exert considerable mental activity, Watson. I would ask you, therefore, to leave me alone until luncheon, when perhaps I will have seen through the mists of obfuscation that surround this affair and come to a conclusion.'

For the next few hours, I felt rather like a fish out of

water. I read the latest edition of *The Avalon Independent* from cover to cover. Then for another while, I gazed mournfully out of the window upon the townsfolk going about their business. Briefly my eye fell upon a young woman going from shop to shop and accumulating various supplies and comestables, shopping list in hand. It occurred to me, that whilst Sherlock Holmes was no more than ten feet away from me, sitting on his bed, knees drawn up together, his hands clasped around them deep in thought and swathed in clouds of blue tobacco smoke, he was mentally performing the same acts, which the young woman was doing physically. My hope was that it would not be too long before his intellectual gymnastics brought him to a judgement.

I wandered into the hotel games room and spent a further hour on the billiards table, playing a lonely solo, one hundred-up. I only wished that my regular playing companion, Thurston, was with me. Then, suddenly, Holmes was standing at my side. He looked flushed, his hands were trembling and there was a glint in his eye.

'You have the answer to this conundrum?' I asked him.

Holmes nodded. 'I have indeed,' he said, as he rubbed his hands briskly together. 'I believe, however, that the luncheon gong has gone. So let us dine first and dwell upon the matter last. I shall merely say for the present that later this afternoon, I will pay a visit on Sergeant Buckland. There are one or two matters I need to discuss with him if we are to be successful in our contrivances.'

Despite my best endeavours, Holmes refused to speak again upon the subject. All I could extract from him was that the forecast was for a frosty night and I should wrap up warmly for our undertaking.

It was well past midnight when Sherlock Holmes and I stepped out at last onto the streets of Glastonbury. We were well wrapped up against the chill night air and the drizzle that seemed to be, more or less, a constant companion in our activities. Holmes, quite as usual, had decided that he would tell me nothing about our movements, save that all would be explained when we arrived at our destination. For myself, I fancied that I knew the identity of our man and even why he was engaged in this series of bizarre crimes.

Sergeant Buckland was waiting by the town cross, and Holmes and the policeman held a brief council of war. Then, at a signal from the sergeant, two constables detached themselves from one of the shop fronts and moved away into the direction of Benedict Street, returning, I supposed, to the police station.

Next, we turned our faces into the wind and walked up the High Street, dimly lit by the public lighting. I nudged Holmes. 'It is hardly surprising that these crimes were so easy to conceal, when it is hard to see more than twenty paces in front of one.'

Our journey proved to be a short one, however, for Holmes quickly led the sergeant and myself across the street, then ushered us down a dimly lit alleyway between two shops.

'Show a light there, Watson,' he said quietly.

I slipped the cover off the dark lantern and the narrow concourse was bathed in its glow. 'Where are we headed for?' I asked Holmes.

'Almost there, old fellow,' he replied.

'Why, this is the rear entrance to Bulleid and Nixon,' I exclaimed.

'Indeed. Here, sooner or later, we will solve at least a part of this mystery.'

He looked over the fence that ran around the back of the property and gave a murmur of satisfaction. 'Ah, our friend is in residence. Now, Sergeant Buckland, I require your assistance, if you please.'

'Certainly, Mr Holmes. What do you wish me to do?'

'In precisely five minutes, I would like you to bang heartily upon the front door of Bulleid and Nixon and announce your presence. You will then return and we shall see what effect the arrival of the police force has on our friend within.'

As the sergeant made his way back along the alleyway, Holmes hoisted himself up and over the fence, then jumped down lightly upon the other side. A moment later his head appeared over the fence. 'Hand me the lantern, there must be a gate along here . . . Ah, here we are,' he laughed.

'What is it, old fellow?'

'The gate does not appear to be locked. Ah well, it will at least save you the climb.'

Quickly I found myself in the yard of Bulleid and Nixon. Holmes closed the gate behind me and slipped the bolt.

'A little insurance, Watson,' he explained.

Then we heard the sound of a heavy hand on the front door of the solicitor's office. Sergeant Buckland was applying himself with a will.

Suddenly, there came a good deal of thumping and bumping from within, followed immediately by a number of footfalls. Holmes glanced quickly at me.

'Ready, Watson?'

'I'm ready.'

Abruptly the rear door was thrown open and two men bolted out. One, a slight young man, came half-jumping, half-stumbling down the steps. He brushed Holmes aside and made for the exit. The other, a tall, well-rounded fellow and considerably less active, was stopped short by Holmes. The first man was by now pulling frantically at the gate in his desire to escape.

'Holmes!' I cried. 'The fellow is getting away.'

He did not get very far, however, for a combination of the gate and the burly form of Sergeant Buckland were blocking his way. There was the briefest of struggles, then the man allowed the policeman to handcuff him without further demur.

The other man, however, was disinclined to struggle. Indeed, he appeared to be quite resigned to his fate and was easily led away. Suddenly the light of my lamp fell upon his face.

'Why, it is Mr Lockyear,' I cried. 'I expected as much.'

Holmes chuckled. 'Quite so, Watson.'

'So you were right, Mr Holmes,' said Sergeant Buckland. 'But who is our friend here?'

The policeman turned his captive to face the light.

'Beck!' I exclaimed. 'What has he to do with this?'

'What indeed,' replied Holmes. 'But our friends here represent only a part of the solution to the mystery.'

Our captives were propelled along the alleyway and out into the street. The policeman blew upon his whistle and two more constables appeared from the shadows of the churchyard.

As the constables led the miscreants away, Holmes smiled briefly. 'Come along, gentlemen, one half of our task is completed, now we must finish the remainder.'

By now the rain had ceased and the moon was peering out from behind the broken clouds. As we retraced our steps, I was somewhat confused. 'Holmes?'

'Yes, my dear fellow?'

'Is this matter now not at an end? What is this two-part task to which you are referring? Who else is concerned with this affair?'

'He is the third man, Watson. Someone neither you nor myself, nor indeed Sergeant Buckland, has ever met. He is the man who holds the key to this mystery.'

'And where are we to find this veritable master mind?' I demanded.

'If you will follow me, my boy. We are about to meet him.'

I sighed. 'Very well, let us proceed.'

We had walked along Benedict Street, almost as far as the police station, when Holmes brought our sojourn to a halt.

'Mr Lockyear's house?' I said.

'Indeed.'

By now the sky had cleared completely and the moon lit up all around. Holmes expressed his satisfaction. 'Excellent,' he said. 'It exactly suits our purpose.'

One of the constables dispatched earlier by Sergeant Buckland was awaiting our arrival.

'Anyone come out?' Sergeant Buckland asked him.

'No, Sergeant. No sign of anybody.'

'Very good, take Sharpe and watch the road.'

The constable saluted and disappeared behind the hedge.

'Now,' said Holmes firmly. 'Let us proceed.'

He produced from an inside pocket his little pouch of tools, picks and instruments, and before too long there came a sharp click from the lock. I noticed with a wry smile that the Sergeant pretended to watch the progress of the moon across the sky during the process.

As we entered the house all was dark, save the shaft of light escaping from under the door at the end of the passage. With Holmes leading the way, our party crept silently along. Holmes turned the knob and the door swung open with only the merest hint of a creak.

The light we had earlier observed came not from this room, but from a wooden and glass lean-to beyond. I was somewhat surprised to discover that of the woodworking machinery there was no sign.

'Mr Lockyear works down in the cellar,' Sergeant Buckland told me.

Suddenly, there came from within the lean-to, the sound of movement. Holmes signalled for us to be silent. Then, from a previously unseen hole in the floor, a man's head appeared. As he rose above ground level, I could see that he was extremely dirty. He stopped for a moment to pull on a rope and very quickly a wooden bucket piled with earth appeared. He unhooked the rope and walked out into the garden where he deposited the soil.

As the man turned and walked back, Holmes gave a sharp intake of breath and pressed Sergeant Buckland and myself back to the kitchen wall. 'I trust, Watson, that your revolver is handy,' he whispered.

I patted the bulge in my coat and nodded. Long experience had taught me that when following Holmes into possible danger it was as well to go fully prepared.

Once more, the man began to disappear back down into the hole from where he had emerged. Holmes stepped out from our place of hiding and opened the kitchen door, which he quickly closed with a bang and proceeded to walk noisily across the room. The sounds had clearly been heard by the man in the hole, because his voice was swiftly heard.

'That you, Jack, old son? You were quick getting old Lockyear settled.'

'It's me,' said Holmes, in a voice which sounded for all the world like Beck's. 'Thought I would get back quick and give you a hand. Find anything of interest?'

A bundle was thrown up from the hole.

'Here, just some old rags and a lump of metal. Apart from that, nothing.'

Holmes picked up the bundle and laid it upon the table. The man in the hole appeared to be correct, there were the remains of what looked to be a leather jerkin, a greenish length of metal and a lump of dirty-looking stone.

Again, the disembodied voice came. 'Come on, Jack. Stop messing with that junk and help a fellow.'

Holmes smiled. It was not a pleasant smile, but it was one with which I was familiar. Usually it was connected with the direst of consequences for someone he had designs upon. 'Here, just a minute,' he said in Beck's voice. 'Come up, I think I've got something to show you.'

From below, there came an amount of grumbling, before the sound of footfalls on the ladder could be heard. Holmes moved over to the hole.

'Funny,' said the man as he climbed the ladder. 'All this digging and still no sign of the stuff. You sure we measured it right, Jack?'

Holmes reached down into the hole with one hand and signalled to the sergeant with the other that he should join him. 'Here, old fellow,' he said to the man, 'let me help you up.'

Suddenly Holmes had the man in a vice-like grip and before he could struggle he was dragged bodily out of the hole and handcuffed.

'Good evening, Mr Wilson Kemp,' said Holmes, coolly. 'How very nice to see you again.'

It was almost two hours after the remarkable events and the surprise revelation that a man, long thought to be dead, had been the prime mover. Sherlock Holmes and I sat in the kitchen of Sergeant Buckland's warming ourselves before his range.

Mrs Buckland, the policeman's lady wife, was, like most sensible people, deep in the arms of Morpheus, but we, who had drunk life to the dregs, were far too buoyed up and intoxicated by our success to sleep. No matter the fact that Sergeant Buckland was expected on duty at seven am and Holmes and I needed to catch the early train to Paddington, we all felt the need for a smoke and a glass of the stuff that warms and cheers before taking to our beds.

A little earlier I had sat at the back of the small police station and observed Holmes and Sergeant Buckland as they interviewed the miscreants.

Beck, for his part, had refused to discuss the matter. Kemp advised Holmes to 'find out', but would say little more, save that he had escaped from a far worse position in Buda-Pest and he would soon be free again in England. Moreover, he would only speak with a senior Scotland Yard officer.

My initial observation of Mr Lockyear, when he was ushered into the room, was just how much the whole episode seemed to have aged him. He sat slumped in the chair and looked at Holmes with hollow eyes. 'You have caught me red-handed, Mr Holmes,' he said, quietly. 'So there is little point in my prevaricating. I am here because of money, nothing more, nothing less.'

Holmes looked keenly at the solicitor's clerk. 'Perhaps you can explain yourself, sir?'

'I am sorry, Mr Holmes. My oath of silence prevents any discussion of the matter, save to say that I am guilty as charged.'

'Those who are not of the body must remain in ignorance,' said Holmes quietly.

Mr Lockyear sat up quite straight in his chair and looked at him with wide eyes. Holmes reached into an inside pocket and took out the sheet of paper upon which he had copied Mr Lockyear's notes. He spread the paper out upon the table.

Holmes looked sharply at the solicitor's clerk. 'Would it surprise you, sir, if I told you that these notes convince me that your crimes were committed as a part of a series of tasks you have been set.'

'You cannot know,' said Mr Lockyear.

Holmes smiled briefly. 'Your first task was to turn around the signposts and turn heads thereby. Not quite going to Hades, eh, Mr Lockyear, but you almost sent others to that delightful spot. Your second task was to steal the blooms from the Glastonbury thorn. Not quite golden apples, but it is hardly the season. Your third task was to take away the sign from the butcher's. Not quite oxen, but beef all the same. Task four was to steal the flag of St George from the hotel. I suppose that the cross belts on the flag were approximate to the Belt of Hippolyta. Your fifth task was to remove all the water from the horse trough. No flesh-eating mares in Glastonbury, Mr Lockyear? Tonight you were to steal from your employers, Bulleid and Nixon. How astute of you to connect them with the capture of the Cretan Bull.'

By now Mr Lockyear was sitting looking at Sherlock Holmes with an open mouth. Holmes, however, was not finished. 'Your next and, I believe, final task, Mr Lockyear, concerned the town's pigeons. How did you intend to kill them? Poisoned grain perhaps?'

The clerk nodded silently.

'Would it help you, sir, if I told you that your friend Wilson Kemp is no puppet-master and that you are the victim of a cruel hoax?' said Holmes gently.

'No,' replied our prisoner. 'It cannot be.'

'I can assure you, Mr Lockyear, that Kemp is a thoroughgoing villain, nothing more, nothing less. He is wanted for crimes as foul as kidnapping, false imprisonment and murder. You owe him nothing, sir.'

Mr Lockyear was silent for a moment. Clearly his mind was turning over the facts Holmes had set before him. He looked in turn at Sergeant Buckland, myself and finally Sherlock Holmes. He seemed to have come to a decision. 'Mr Holmes, I shall tell you everything. But first I imagine that you would care to understand exactly how I came to get myself in this horrible position?'

Holmes said nothing, but he nodded his agreement.

'I am a widower of many seasons. We had a daughter, but she is also dead these three years; but I really lost my daughter some fourteen years ago, when after a serious disagreement she moved away, I know not where. Apparently she also had a daughter, but I knew nothing of that until her death. The child was born out of wedlock and I suppose that she was too concerned about my reaction to tell me.

'It was decided, therefore, that the girl would be placed in an orphanage, but I managed to convince the authorities that she would be better cared for under my protection. Accordingly, I arranged for her to stay with a cousin on my wife's side of the family, and although I absolved myself from her upbringing I have promised to support her financially.

'As you can imagine, Mr Holmes, my salary as an articled clerk for Mr Bulleid is not exactly worth a king's ransom, but it has kept me comfortable. The added financial strain of the upkeep of my granddaughter has cost me dear. I have a year to go before my retirement and there is nothing for me to fall back upon, yet the child will need to be supported for several more years.

'It was about three months ago when I was at the height of my misery, my housekeeper, Mrs White, came in and told me that she had heard about a Mr Beck who was presently seeking accommodation. He had earlier in the day placed a notice in the newsagent's window. Very quickly I tracked him down to a small hotel and we discussed the matter. He said that he was a travelling salesman and would be away from his lodgings on and off, so he wouldn't be much trouble to me.

'He seemed to be exactly the kind of fellow I needed. We agreed a price and he was invited to move in at his earliest convenience. It seemed that my money problems, if not solved, were to become ameliorated.

'After a week or so, Beck told me about his particular interest in local history. I told him that in Glastonbury there are any number of myths and legends. Indeed quite recently there has been something of a find at Chalybeate Spa, where a fellow is reported to have discovered a blue glass vessel. He claims it was something to do with the supposed visit of Joseph of Arimethea to England after the death of Christ. He told me that someone had mentioned that the remains of an ancient King of England were to be found somewhere in the area. I laughed and said that tales of Arthur simply abounded. He said, no it was not Arthur, but he didn't know who it was.

'Well, the matter was dropped for a little while, then one night Beck came to me and said that his brother was coming to Glastonbury and would I mind accommodating him, same terms? Thinking that the extra money would be welcome, I agreed.

'When his brother arrived, he seemed to be a fellow of a very different mind. He was well dressed, wore expensive rings and had an air of authority about him. He asked me to call him Will. Like his brother, he was interested in the legends of Glastonbury and soon we three fell to talking about them and mythology in general.

'Then just about three weeks ago, I accidentally disturbed Will as he was dressing. He was off to some function and I was going to offer him my best cufflinks. He was dressed in the most remarkable waistcoat. It was made up from the flag of St George and it had a kind of shield, which had "The Sons of Hercules" upon it. Will didn't seem too happy to see me, he bolted back into his room and shut the door.

'I have to say that my interest was piqued. Well, the very next evening when I returned from my employment, it was satiated. Beck and Will were waiting in the kitchen for me. I immediately apologized to Will for embarrassing him. He said that it was all his fault and I deserved an explanation. The two looked at each other and, as if a decision had just been come to, they proceeded to tell me all about a society to which they both belonged, "The Sons of Hercules".

'Will was a senior figure from the third circle, whilst Beck was only on the first level. The society resembled the Freemasons in its secrecy, but had a pedigree of a far greater age. Will said that membership was a route to great influence and wealth. He then told me that several members of the aristocracy were highly placed and had been so for generations.'

Mr Lockyear looked at the paper Holmes had placed before him. 'These are the notes I made when I was given my first instructions as a neophyte. Will said that I was exactly the type of fellow who would flourish in the society. At first, I was concerned that I would be required to pay an initiation fee. Beck laughed. He said that money was not even considered. There was, however, as an initiation, a series of tasks I would have to perform. Tasks that would be of a fashion that would cause comment in the community, but would cause no harm to anyone.

'To be quite honest, Mr Holmes, I saw the real possibility of getting out of my present financial strife. Will had evidence of his personal riches brought about by his association with the society and he asked Beck to go up and get his war chest, as he called it. When I saw the contents, I would have no doubts about the power of the society.

'Beck came back a few moments later. He was carrying a small wooden casket. He placed it upon the table before me and Will opened it. Well, Mr Holmes, the casket was crammed with golden sovereigns. Will invited me to count them. There were exactly two hundred. What more proof did I require? I was enrolled; only the series of tests now stood before me and riches beyond my wildest dreams.'

'Let me see,' said Holmes languidly, referring once more to the paper on the table. "Sun, Moon, Tura, Woden, Thor,

Frier, Saturn". If we add the word "day" after each, then we have the original names of the days of the week.'

— 'Quite so,' agreed Mr Lockyear. 'I had also to memorize the levels of attainment and the mantra the membership was expected to chant. Will then told me about the first task he had set me. I had to turn the signposts around. The rest you know, Mr Holmes.'

The old fellow sighed heavily and shook his head. I looked at Sherlock Holmes. This was no evil man. Certainly, he was a fool of the highest order and his dreams of personal wealth had been dashed on the rocks of reality. His crimes had also forced possible ruination of the future of his grandchild. An innocent caught up in this web of intrigue.

Holmes looked back at me and signalled that I should remain silent. He stood up and thanked Mr Lockyear for his candidness and invited Sergeant Buckland to return his guest to the cells. He sighed. 'Well now, Watson. Beck said that we should "find out" why he and Wilson were so fascinated by the ground under Mr Lockyear's house. I suggest, therefore, that we take him up on his kind offer.'

A few moments later, Holmes led me into the home of Mr Lockyear once more. On this occasion, however, he used the door key. Once in the kitchen, he lit the lamp earlier used by Wilson. I stood peering down the hole.

'I suppose that the Sons of Hercules is a bogus organization?' I said, thoughtfully.

'A mere artifice intended to entrap the unwary,' he agreed.

'But what lies behind it all?'

Holmes came over and looked down the hole as well.

'Here is the reason,' he said. 'They were keeping Mr Lockyear occupied, whilst they worked unhindered here.

The earth of the excavation has no doubt been spread upon the garden. Who would notice it at this time of year, when the days are so short? Then, when it was time for Mr Lockyear's return, perhaps some three hours later, they would have the boards back over the hole and everything would appear to be quite as usual.'

'But for how long did they expect to keep the charade going?' I asked. 'They could hardly keep on sending the old fellow out on tasks *ad infinitum*.'

'Indeed,' he agreed. 'I believe that it was their expectation that the task would quickly be completed and then they would simply fold their tents and disappear into the night, leaving their victim high and dry.'

'What of the casket full of gold?' I said, suddenly recalling Mr Lockyear's confession. 'There was no opportunity for the villains to remove it, so it must still be somewhere in the house.'

'Excellent, Watson. Let us satisfy our curiosity on the matter.'

Upstairs, we virtually ransacked the three bedrooms. Eventually, however, we came across the prize we were seeking. Holmes pulled out one of the beds and there on the floor lay a bundle of old clothes. Holmes unwrapped the rags and there was the casket. 'Now, Watson, let us see the riches of Croesus.'

He opened the box and the glint of gold was quickly apparent.

'Good heavens, Mr Lockyear was not exaggerating,' I cried.

Holmes made no comment; instead he took a coin from the pile and looked carefully at it. Then he weighed it in his hand. A noise of disgust emanated from his lips. 'Pah! Pinchbeck!'

'It cannot be,' I exclaimed.

Holmes looked at me, his eyes were like gimlets. 'Watson, I believe it was you, yourself, when writing so eloquently about my merits and demerits many years ago, described me as possessing a considerable knowledge of metallurgy. So please believe that when I inform you that this is pinchbeck, pinchbeck it is.'

I sighed, poor Mr Lockyear. Duplicity heaped upon duplicity.

A warm, if pale, sun was shining out of a clear blue sky as the train rattled and bumped along between Glastonbury and Bath. Sherlock Holmes and I were returning to our rooms in Baker Street, to prepare for the appointment with Inspector Lestrade and his mysterious client. There had just been sufficient time for us to witness the committal proceedings of Wilson Kemp and John 'Beck' Beckton and Edgar Lockyear. Holmes had generously spoken up for Mr Lockyear and had convinced the magistrate that the old man was more sinned against, than a sinner. He said that Kemp and Beckton were thoroughly unpleasant characters and Kemp in particular was a villain of the worst sort and was still wanted by the authorities in connection with a murder some five years earlier.

As a result of Holmes's intervention on his behalf, Mr Lockyear was bound over for twelve months, with the sum of £100 to be paid only if he was brought before the court for any reason at all. As for the villains, Kemp and Beckton, they were committed to the assizes for trial and almost certain imprisonment.

Holmes lay back in his seat and stretched his legs before him. He looked keenly at me making my notes on the events of the last few days. 'You are very industrious,' he remarked.

'The complexity of the matter makes it necessary for me to set the facts down now, rather than leaving it for later. I may add, Holmes, that there are one or two points you may care to explain for me.'

'If I can be of service, Watson.'

I gazed at my list of questions, appended in the margins of my notes. 'Well now. Why did you keep from Mr Lockyear the fact that his notebook had been found, not as he supposed in the street, but up on the roof of the hotel?'

'It was clear to me that even such an obtuse fellow as Edgar Lockyear would have realized that his misdemeanours had come to light.'

'And surely the affair would have ended there?' I objected.

'So it would,' Holmes agreed. 'But what was lying at the back of these crimes would never have come to light. Last evening I would not have been in a position to confuse my enemies. Mr Lockyear, duty-bound by his oath, would have remained silent and the real criminals would have escaped scot free.'

I sighed. 'Perhaps you are right.'

'Indeed, the intellectual drive for these events clearly did not lie with Mr Lockyear. Someone else was pulling the strings. The old fellow left too many clues to his involvement. The spiral of wood in the trunk of the thorn, the careless loss of his notebook, the tin cup used to remove the water from the horse trough tied up with solicitor's pink ribbon. These were elementary errors perpetrated by a catspaw in someone else's game.'

'What of the Sons of Hercules?' I said. 'I perceive that it

was something unconsciously said by myself, which set your mind on its final route.'

Holmes laughed. 'It was when you described the tasks performed by the miscreant as "positively Herculean" that the prospects of a secret society came into my mind. You will recall that, earlier in our investigation, I had been convinced that there was a common thread running through the affair. It was your intervention, my dear fellow, which gave me the vital clue. When, later, I turned my mind to the matter, I was considerably assisted by the volume *Tales of Ancient Greece and Ancient Rome* by R.A. Gibson, borrowed from the bookshelf of Mr Poole. I looked up the twelve labours of Hercules and there was the answer.

'It was not quite a simple task, for I had to transpose the modern trials of Mr Lockyear and make them fit the ancient ones of Hercules. I only discovered the exact relationship, however, by reversing them. Thus I was able to predict the visit of Mr Lockyear to the premises of Mr Bulleid, his employer, and later inform him about his next engagement.'

I continued to write for a few moments, then, as I looked up for inspiration, I saw Holmes watching me and smiling. 'Do you wish to know exactly how it came to pass that Kemp and Beckton came to be under Mr Lockyear's roof in the first place?'

'Indeed, it seems to be particularly coincidental that Beckton just happened to be looking for lodgings at the right time. I suppose that he was lucky that the old boy happened to be on the lookout for a lodger?'

'Quite so. Once securely ensconced they had to get him out of the house for a goodly period of time. It was no use digging whilst he was at his woodworking because he could have surprised them at any time. So they invented this whole feast of fandangles to keep him occupied.'

'Have you any notion for what it was they were so diligently searching? For I perceive that they were not digging a huge hole in Mr Lockyear's lean-to for the exercise it afforded them.'

'No, indeed,' said Holmes, taking a cream-coloured and rather crumpled-looking object from his pocket. 'This parchment tells me that there is an ancient treasure-trove hidden beneath a certain marker stone on the road between Glastonbury and the hamlet of Street. Judging by the style and content, I imagine it to be from late Tudor times. It describes the exact spot where this treasure can be found. It is doubtless clear to you that it is the house of Mr Lockyear under which it is hidden.'

'But how did this parchment come into your hands?' I cried.

'Oh,' said Holmes, 'it was hidden beneath the counterfeit sovereigns.'

I smiled and shook my head. 'So it was this "treasure map" which has been the cause of so much trouble,' I said. 'Do you suppose it to be genuine, Holmes?'

'I do not for a moment imagine it to be anything but genuine.'

'Then why did they not find what they were seeking?'

Holmes reached out and opened his gladstone. 'They found what they were seeking, my boy, only they did not know it.'

'Good heavens!'

I watched with ardent interest as he removed something from his bag.

'Why, it is the old bundle discarded by Kemp last night.'

'Indeed,' said Holmes, as he unfurled the worn and ragged leather jerkin, once again revealing the greenish metal and the concretion which once had been a brooch, perhaps. 'Although Kemp and Beckton had greed on their side, they had no knowledge of ancient relics. They fondly believed that anything hidden away would remain as pristine as the day it was buried. This is the treasure they have done so much to obtain; and they have discarded it without a second thought.'

'What do you make of it?'

'I believe the objects to be the jerkin, the sword and the neck clasp of King Alfred, hidden after his defeat at the hands of the Danes, with the intention of reclaiming them when matters became more favourable once more. Perhaps knowledge of their existence became lost or forgotten to most men. Yet as we can see, someone kept it in memory, at least until the fifteenth century. I believe these objects to be genuine, Watson. I would stake my reputation upon it.'

I blew out my cheeks and rubbed my chin reflectively. 'Men are strange creatures, Holmes. Some move heaven and earth to obtain their desire; others, it seems, will move only earth.'

A Voice from the Ether

In the year 1893, I wrote with great feeling about the disappearance and presumed death of Sherlock Holmes. At the time my grief for the loss of my friend was quite overwhelming and complete. Now, after the passing of three years and the return of the great man, I have recalled to mind the factual errors in my account of his (then) last case published as 'The Final Problem'. I had then indicated that this was our only adventure together in that year, but the absolute truth is, in late February, Holmes was called upon to solve a matter in which his strong deductive and intuitive powers were stretched to their absolute maximum. A case, by the greatest of coincidences, which involved a man who, only a few months earlier, Sherlock Holmes had assisted in a most remarkable way, and another man whose involvement with a criminal mastermind almost ended in a terrible and tragic conclusion.

I had been expecting Sherlock Holmes for some considerable time. On at least three occasions I took out my watch to check it. He was certainly very late and getting later. Mrs Hudson had kindly brought me a cup of tea, but before too long I began to fidget. Then at last I heard his footsteps on the stairs.

The door burst open. It was indeed Holmes. He was carrying a very large polished wooden box.

'My dear fellow,' he said, 'I am so sorry to have kept you waiting. Would you mind clearing a space on the table so I may be relieved of my burden?'

Jumping up, I quickly moved several piles of newspapers and two large leather-bound volumes, which Holmes no doubt intended to add to his vast library of cuttings.

'What on earth have you got there?' I said. 'A new microscope, perhaps?'

Holmes smiled his quick smile as he unfastened the metal clasps on each side of the box. Raising the lid, he replied with a question of his own. 'There, my boy. What do you make of this?'

I looked for some moments at the machine he had exposed. At first sight, it resembled a sewing machine. It had a roller surmounted by a strange elbow-shaped fitment, which could be rocked back and forth, enabling it to come into contact with the roller. 'My dear fellow,' I said, 'I have absolutely no idea. What is this contraption for?'

Holmes smiled in benign superiority. 'This contraption, as you so elegantly put it, Watson, is a phonograph.'

'Edison's phonograph?'

Holmes nodded. 'The very same.'

'I have never seen one before. What is its purpose?'

'It is presently used by business people chiefly as an *aide memoire*. Senior members of staff will leave messages on it for their juniors, or for later reference.'

Hanging up his overcoat, Holmes produced from his pockets six cardboard tubes with metal lids. 'Would you care to see, or should I say, hear how it is done?'

'Indeed.'

'I will have to wire the machine up first,' he said.

Opening a concealed door in the wooden base, Holmes

pulled out a battery and connected it to two wires hidden in the compartment. From his jacket pocket he produced a brass trumpet, which he proceeded to screw into the elbow-shaped fitment. 'Now,' he said, 'for the cylinder.'

Taking one of the tubes, Holmes flipped off the lid. The cylinder he extracted was dark and smooth. He slipped it over the roller and set the elbow-shaped fitment over it. 'Now, Watson. I would like you to say something into this trumpet. Speak quite loudly and clearly and be prepared for a surprise.'

'But what shall I say?' I asked.

Holmes laughed. 'A writer lost for words. Shame on you, Doctor. Come now, you will think of something.'

With that, he flicked a lever and the cylinder began to rotate.

'This is Dr John Watson . . .' I gasped, '. . . of 221B Baker Street . . . I bring you greetings . . . That is all.'

I made a hasty sign to Holmes and he once more flicked the lever, then smiled. 'There you are, my boy, your first recording.'

He pulled away the arm and reset the cylinder. 'Now, let us hear how you sound.'

Once more the machine sprang into life. There was a hissing and crackling, then . . . the sound of a voice.

'This is Dr John Watson . . . of 221B Baker Street . . . I bring you greetings . . . That is all.'

I looked wildly at Sherlock Holmes. He seemed to be amused.

'That was I?' I cried.

'Indeed.'

'But I sounded so . . .' I mentally sought out the appropriate word 'so odd'. I looked doubtfully at Holmes.

'I suppose this is not some kind of an artifice, where you employ someone with an odd-sounding voice to impersonate your victim?'

Holmes slipped the tube off the machine and handed it to me. 'I assure you, Watson, it is the sound of your own voice. Indeed, it does if anything, flatter you slightly.'

I inspected the cylinder. There were grooves cut into its surface where none had previously existed. 'Then it is true. I do sound like that.'

'I would not alarm yourself, Watson,' Holmes said, soothingly. 'It is always something of a shock to hear one's own voice when it is reproduced mechanically. I'm afraid the voice we hear inside our head bears little resemblance to the actual voice everyone else hears.'

'It is a frightful disappointment all the same,' I said, gloomily.

There came the sound of footsteps on the stairs. Holmes stood up. 'Ah, it is Mrs Hudson with the tea. Let us put aside these childish things until later. Then over tea you must tell me what it is that brings you here today.'

During tea I explained that my visit had been brought about by my wife's sudden departure from the matrimonial home. Her old friend, Mrs Whitney, had been taken ill and she had decided to spend a few days with her, whilst she convalesced.

'So you see, Holmes, I am presently at something of a loose end. My practice takes up much of my day, but the nights are distinctly dreary.'

'And you were wondering if you might temporarily resume your tenancy?' said Holmes.

'Exactly.'

'My dear Watson, that would be excellent. You may

come when you like and stay for as long as you wish.'

'Then I shall return home this instant, pack a bag and rejoin you in time for supper!' I cried.

'Capital,' said Holmes. 'Capital.'

It was later the same evening when Holmes and I returned to the subject of the phonograph. Mrs Hudson had cleared away the supper things and we were enjoying a pipe.

'Tell me, Holmes. How did you come by that machine?'

Sherlock Holmes paused for a brief moment to relight his pipe. 'As you know, Watson, I have recently been retained by Her Majesty's government on a case involving a very clever forger who had insinuated himself into the Bank of England. The matter also involved the Foreign Office and one of the great powers. Well, today, I witnessed the miscreant receiving his just deserts at the Central Criminal Courts.

'Realizing I was running decidedly late, I decided to take the underground, and as it is only a short walk from Giltspur Street to Aldersgate, I decided to proceed along that particular avenue. As I made my hurried way to my destination, a man stepped out from a shop doorway and stood squarely in my way.

' "Good afternoon, Mr Holmes," he said. The florid face and flaming red hair of my interlocutor made him instantly recognizable.

' "Why, it is Mr Jabez Wilson."

' "None other, sir."

'It was only then, Watson, when I realized that in my haste I had failed to notice my route had taken me into Saxe Coburg Square.

' "Good day to you, Mr Wilson," I said. Pointing to the

young man busily sweeping the shop floor behind him, "I hope your new assistant is somewhat more reliable than his predecessor?"

' "Indeed, sir. The reward from the City and Suburban Bank, which you so kindly allowed to come to me, has enabled me to pay full wages on this occasion."

'He suddenly looked a little abashed. Then, clearing his throat, he said, "Mr Holmes, for some little time it has bothered me that I have not been able to make some little . . . hm . . . restitution to your good self. After all, you were able to clear up a nasty situation, sir, very nasty." I waved my hand in a gesture of self-deprecation.

' "It was nothing, Mr Wilson. A mere bagatelle."

' "That is as maybe to you, Mr Holmes, but to me . . ." He paused for a moment, then, as if making up his mind, he blurted out, "I believe I have something from my stock that might suit you. Would you be so kind as to step into the shop and take a look?"

'I sighed quietly, Watson. It seemed to me that a seedy establishment such as Mr Wilson's pawn shop would be very unlikely to contain anything of the remotest interest. Well, imagine my astonishment when, from under the counter, he produced the very machine that is presently sitting on our table.

' "There you are, Mr Holmes," he said, beaming at me. "A nice little toy for the enquiring mind. Will you have it?"

' "Indeed," I replied, much surprised and delighted, "if you will let me."

' "Then take it, Mr Holmes. Take it with the compliments of Jabez Wilson."

'So there you are, Watson. Mr Wilson's debt of honour, paid in full.'

'Quite remarkable,' I said.

Laying down my pipe, I reached behind me for one of the cardboard tubes that lay on the table. 'Why, Holmes,' I remarked, as I opened the tube and tipped out the cylinder, 'this one appears to have been partly used.'

Quickly, I stood up and opened the remaining tubes and inspected the contents. 'Why, all the cylinders are used.'

Holmes knocked out his pipe on the fire-dog and inspected the stem. 'Um . . . I expect so. It is a second-hand machine.'

He stood up and walked over to the table. 'I believe there is a small implement somewhere in the box, which is for shaving the wax, so the cylinder may be re-used.'

He opened another drawer. 'Ah, just as I thought, and look, Watson, headphones. There you are, Doctor. For your exclusive use when you desire to make private notes, which only you need to hear relayed.'

I grunted. 'I have no notes I do not wish you to hear, Holmes. Private or otherwise.'

Holmes slipped a cylinder over the roller and set the machine in motion.

'Surely you are not intent on listening to the confidential thoughts of others?' I objected.

'Private or not, Watson, the unguarded remarks of those foolish enough to part with them fall easy prey for the prying eye, or should I say the prying ear, of the consulting detective.'

Throwing down the empty tube I had been casually inspecting, I declared hotly, 'You may pry if you wish, Holmes. For my part, I have no desire to do so.'

Holmes, quite unperturbed by my outburst, placed the arm onto the spinning cylinder. 'It is as you like it, Watson. I shall call you when I am done.'

I was half-way across the room, when my progress was halted by a voice from the ether.

'. . . My God, they are here. They have found me.'

It was the voice of a man, and he was almost incoherent with fear. 'It is Porritt and Clark. They will kill me for sure . . .'

The man's words were interrupted by a crashing noise and the sound of other voices, indistinct and almost inaudible. There came a second burst of noise, then the machine stopped and silence reigned.

For a moment I stood rooted to the spot. Something quite awful seemed to have happened to the author of those terrible words.

'Great Scott, Holmes!' I cried. 'Are we witnesses to a murder?' Sherlock Holmes looked grim.

'It would seem so, Doctor. It would seem so.'

There have been very few times in my life when I have felt the need for a stiff drink. On this occasion, however, a stimulant was most certainly in order. Working so very intimately with Sherlock Holmes, one expected to be invited to attend at the scene of a crime where the remains of some unfortunate had to be examined. As a doctor, I had often been asked to ascertain the time of, and the reason for, death. But never before had I encountered the act of dying in such an immediate and appalling fashion. Even in Afghanistan, death had been an essentially private affair, when, often as not, it would come from a distance, and be discovered post mortem. But now . . .

Holmes slipped the cylinder from the roller and inspected it closely. 'Look at this, Watson. This must be the cylinder you first inspected. The groove is cut only slightly more than half-way along the wax. And see here . . . it ends abruptly and somewhat unevenly.'

'As if the arm had been suddenly knocked away?'

'Exactly.'

Holmes held the cylinder up for my inspection. 'There is also a number scratched into the wax . . . five.'

Quickly he examined the other cylinders. Each was inscribed with a number. Holmes then rearranged them in order. He slipped the cylinder numbered '1' over the roller.

'Now,' he said, starting up the machine once more, 'perhaps we may get to the heart of the matter.'

The machine crackled into life and for the next fifteen minutes, Sherlock Holmes and I listened to the most extraordinary last will and testament of a condemned man which, I believe, the world has ever, or indeed will ever, hear. I now produce a word-for-word transcription.

'My name is Tom George . . . The next few days could prove to be the last of my life. And if it is to be so, I need to leave a message explaining the events which have brought such retribution upon my head.

'Nearly fourteen years ago I joined forces with three others and between us we formed a gang. Truthfully, we were a gang of robbers and common footpads. Over a period of five years, we became quite wealthy on our ill-gotten gains. Then, one day on Blackheath the police fell upon us and we were taken away for trial and inevitable incarceration. My companions, Wilson Porritt, John Gool and Joseph Clark and I, were taken before the courts and charged with dozens of crimes. It was then I decided to turn Queen's evidence and save my own skin. As a result, my companions received thirteen years' hard labour, while for my part, I was sent down for three years.

'Just as the others were being taken away to begin their sentences, Wilson Porritt broke free from his captors and rushed back into the court. Grabbing me by the collar, he cried, "Traitor! You may have sent me down for thirteen years, but you shall live to regret it! You see if you don't!"

'Even from the entrance to the cells down below, I could still hear him shouting, "Keep looking over your shoulder, Tom George. One day I'll have my revenge."

'At first, I believed his outburst to be no more than him venting his spleen. Then, six months into my prison sentence, I received a note smuggled to me when I was on a work party. It was from Porritt and simply read, "Tom, we have not forgotten you. Keep looking over your shoulder." It was then, when I realized Wilson Porritt had meant exactly what he had said. All I could hope for was the possibility that, over time, he would mellow.

'But I was wrong. Over the next three years I received several more notes in the same vein from him. Then, at last, my time for release came. I was relieved. Now I would be free of my persecutor. Yet, when I collected my belongings, I found a note pinned to the bag. It read:

' "Tom, you are now going out. You have served a traitor's sentence. We have ten years to do, but one day, Tom. One day, we shall be free. Don't think you'll get away with it because you won't. Wherever you go, Tom, I'll find you, so keep looking over your shoulder. W.P."

'A cold shiver ran down my spine. I thanked heaven that for the foreseeable future I would be free from Porritt and his threats. Of the next few years, there is little enough to tell. Prison is a terrible place and I had no desire to go back there. Instead I returned to my old trade of carpentry. Even when times were hard, I kept to the straight and narrow. Indeed, after a few years I had even managed to put a little aside for a rainy day. But all the time the brooding presence of Wilson Porritt hung over me like an old black cloud. So, as a consequence, I moved around quite a lot seeking any work I could get. Then five years ago, I gained employment as a dockyard carpenter and just over a year ago an unfinished ship was sent to sea on a voyage to Egypt and the Sudan. I was asked to join up to finish the job *in situ*.

'In Egypt I saw the famous sights of antiquity. The pyramids, the Sphinx and the great temples of the Kings. It was there I discovered, quite by accident, a golden bracelet almost completely buried in the sand. Quickly, I hid the treasure in my shirt and made my way back to the ship.

'All throughout the remainder of the voyage, I guarded my find jealously. On my return to England, I made my way to Limehouse, to see a man whom, in my days as a felon, I had often dealt with. We all knew him as Maury Attlee. Of course, it was an alias, indeed, he was known all over the country by a number of names. Attlee soon put me on the right road moneywise. My golden bracelet fetched three hundred pounds.

'While we were squaring away the deal, Attlee told me that John Gool had died in prison. He also told me that Porritt and Clark were out. They had been released early on a good behaviour bond. Knowing full well Attlee's importance in the underworld of crime, Porritt had immediately gone to see him, asking of news about me. He expected Porritt to return shortly, but I should not worry. Attlee would tell him nothing of our business. But I didn't trust him.

'So I came back here to my shack on the island and decided to pack up my things and move on. Foolishly, I had told Attlee my recent history and I knew that I would not be safe for very long. Then I realized that running away would be useless. The money I had raised from the sale of the bracelet would not last for ever and one day I would need to resurface. I could be sure that it would not be too long before my persecutors found me once more. So I have decided to just wait. I am quite sure that Attlee has told them of my whereabouts. When they come, as they will, I shall offer them some of the money. Perhaps they will accept it as recompense . . . then again, perhaps not.'

The machine ground to a halt. The cylinder had run to its completion. Sherlock Holmes picked up the fifth and final tube.

'Well, now, Watson,' he said. 'The final act of a one-man play. We have previously heard some of the last cylinder. Now we shall hear all.'

Once more the machine whirred into life. The voice of Tom George again filled the room. Now, however, there was a strong sense of urgency in his tone.

'Porritt is here, so is Clark. I saw them on the mainland earlier this morning. I have my letters delivered to the Swan Hotel. Mrs Nicholson takes them in for me. Unfortunately, they were in the saloon when I walked into the hotel.

' "Tom!" said Porritt. "At long last we have found you."

'Clark said nothing. He just smiled. Then he grabbed my arm. "Look," I said, "I know you have good cause to hate me. I was a coward. But I have some money. I know it will be little enough to pay you back for the years you were inside, but it might help some."

'Porritt looked at Clark, then at me. He smiled his evil smile. "How much?"

' "About three hundred pounds."

' "Three hundred?" he cried in surprise.

' "Or thereabouts," I said.

'They looked at each other and something seemed to pass between them. I knew at once that my life was in the gravest danger. They would have the money and they would also have me. I had to act at once. So I head-butted Clark, who fell into Wilson. In the uproar I took to my heels and ran. Through the little streets I raced. As I ran, I could hear them behind me. Thankfully my years of activity were in contrast to the sedentary lives of my enemies and I managed to lose them. I doubled back to the Swan. There I jumped upon my bicycle and rode away as quickly as I could. Through the country lanes I rode pell-mell, then over to the island. The tide was rising over the causeway and I knew that very soon I would once again be cut off from the world, safe for the time being from Porritt and Clark.

'But now the tide has receded and at any moment I expect a knock on the door. I don't suppose I shall have too long to wait so I now set down my whereabouts so that the crime my enemies are soon to commit will not go unheeded or unpunished . . . My God, they are here. They have found me . . . It is Porritt and Clark. They will kill me for sure . . .'

Once more there came the crashing noise, interrupting Tom George's testament. The machine stopped and there was silence in the room.

Rather shaken, I took a deep breath. I looked at my companion. Even the normally imperturbable Sherlock

Holmes appeared moved by the dark and terrible narrative of Tom George.

'Is there anything we can do for the poor fellow, Holmes?'

'Other than saying a prayer for his immortal soul, Watson, I think not.'

'But surely, it may not be too late to intervene?' I objected.

'To do that, my dear fellow, we firstly need to discover his whereabouts. Unfortunately, his assailants have prevented him from telling us.' Holmes smiled his little tight smile. 'However, I believe there are sufficient clues in his testament for us, if not to save Tom George from his fate, then to ensure his final wishes, that his persecutors do not go unpunished, are obeyed. So put away that long face, Watson. We shall work it out, we shall work it out.'

It was very early the next morning when I rose from my bed. I had spent a quite wretched night. Sleep, when it came, was a fitful affair interrupted as it was by dreams of haggard prisoners chained together in long straggling lines; of evil-looking men silently stalking me and of water lapping all around and slowly engulfing me.

I checked my watch. It was barely six-thirty. Holmes, I imagined, would not yet be abroad, so I was surprised to find him hard at work. 'My dear fellow,' I cried, my eyes watering in the smoke-filled atmosphere, 'surely you have not been up all night?'

Holmes took out his watch and looked at it absently. 'It would seem so, Watson.'

I watched him as he searched among the debris of papers on the table. 'Have you been able to glean anything useful from the cylinders?' I asked, throwing open the windows to let in the early morning air.

'Possibly, Doctor. Possibly,' he said, enigmatically, as he tidied the sheets of foolscap before him. 'At any rate I have listened closely to the recordings and I have made several notes. Now!' he said briskly, 'Mrs Hudson should be up and about by now. If you would kindly ring for some hot water, Watson, we shall make a start on the day's activities.'

It was a little after eight o'clock when Sherlock Holmes and I stepped down from a cab at the corner of Saxe Coburg Square. Almost at once, I espied the shop of Mr Jabez Wilson. Before us lay the well-remembered shabby-genteel aspect, where four lines of dingy two-storeyed houses enclosed the square. There also was the man himself, lifting the blinds on his shop. His flaming red hair stood out clearly even at a distance and through the smoke-laden atmosphere which pervades this part of the city.

'Why, Mr Holmes, again,' he said, beaming, his little bright eyes almost disappearing beneath the rolls of fat around his pink face. 'And Dr Watson, too. How delightful.'

Holmes came to the point at once. 'Mr Wilson, it is imperative that you inform me exactly when and how you came by the phonograph you presented to me yesterday.'

'Oh dear, Mr Holmes, I hope there is nothing wrong with the machine?'

'It is working admirably, thank you. However, I need to know from whom you obtained it.'

Mr Jabez Wilson signalled us to follow him into his shop. As I had never before set foot over the threshold, I took the opportunity to look around. The premises were very much as Holmes had described them. Shabby, pokey and decidedly overcrowded.

Mr Wilson took down an enormous ledger from a shelf behind the counter. 'Now, let me see,' he said, as he quickly scanned the pages.

'Ah yes, it was brought in last Wednesday. By two gentlemen. I gave them two pounds.'

'There was no pledge?'

'No, Mr Holmes. It was a straight sale.'

'Is that not an uncommon transaction?'

'Indeed, sir, it is. But as I recall, the gentlemen were keen to be relieved of their burden and make a little money into the bargain.'

Holmes rubbed his chin thoughtfully. 'Are you able to describe these "gentlemen", Mr Wilson?'

'Why yes, Mr Holmes. They were both about five and forty. One of 'em I remember particularly because of his funny twisted smile.'

'Hm . . . did they give you their names?'

'Well . . . they called themselves Mr Thomas and Mr George.'

I thought for a brief moment that Sherlock Holmes would explode with anger. He, however, immediately controlled himself. 'Now, Mr Wilson. This is of particular importance. Did they indicate from whence they had come and where they were going?'

Jabez Wilson scratched his head thoughtfully. 'Well, in a manner of speaking, sir. They said they had come from the station and were on their way to one of the banks in High Holborn.'

'Did they now?' said Holmes, narrowing his eyes. He slapped his leg with his gloves. 'Thank you for your assistance, Mr Wilson. Come, Watson. We have much to do.'

'Good day, Mr Wilson!' I cried, as I hurriedly followed

the swiftly departing figure of Sherlock Holmes. 'Thank you for your time.'

Moments later we turned into the busy thoroughfare to the east of Saxe Coburg Square. Holmes hailed a cab and very soon we were clattering through the city's busy streets.

As the cab pulled up outside 221B Baker Street, I stepped down, but Holmes made no attempt to follow me. Instead, he leaned forward and spoke to me in an earnest voice. 'Please listen carefully, Watson. You must go upstairs and pack two overnight bags.' He handed me a piece of paper with a few lines scribbled on it. 'Take this to the telegraph office and send the contents to my friend, Inspector Patterson, at Scotland Yard. He will understand them exactly.'

'Of course, Holmes,' I said.

'In the meantime, I have a little errand to run. I should be no longer than one hour, so please be ready for my return.'

Quickly, I obeyed my instructor. Packing, as far as I was concerned, took only a few minutes. Indeed, my bag had hardly been unpacked. I duly made my way to the telegraph office and sent the following message:

PATTERSON. OUR MAN HAS RESURFACED AND IS MOST
CERTAINLY INVOLVED IN HIS OLD ACTIVITIES.
HE HAS RETURNED TO LIMEHOUSE WITH HIS GANG.
GOOD LUCK. HOLMES.

Upon my return to 221B Baker Street, I pondered upon the events of the last twelve hours and about Holmes's plan of action. It was not too long, however, before the man himself appeared and once more we had taken to the busy streets of the capital.

'Where to, sir?' asked the cabby.

'Liverpool Street Station, if you please,' cried Holmes.

'Liverpool Street?' I said, in some surprise.

'Indeed.'

'Then where are we bound?'

'To Witham, then to Maldon.'

'You believe Tom George is to be found in Maldon?' I said.

'I do not believe it, Doctor,' he said firmly, 'I know it.'

In a little less than half an hour, Sherlock Holmes and I had secured a first-class smoker on the Great Eastern Line to the Essex town. I was full of questions. In particular, I wished to know why it was to Maldon we were now travelling.

Holmes reached into an inside pocket and took out several sheets of paper. On them were the same notes on which he had spent most of the previous night working. There was a mischievous twinkle in his eye. 'Now, my boy. Last night we discovered several important facts about Tom George.'

'Indeed,' I replied. 'He has been in prison, he has spent most of the last few years as a ship's carpenter and he had been trailed by two completely ruthless villains who were bent on making an end to him.'

Holmes looked sharply at me. 'That is commonplace and general information. It is quite irrelevant to the matter in hand.'

A little nettled by the sharpness of his tone, I demanded to know what particular information Holmes had gleaned. He looked benignly at me. 'Let me see now. We know that George lived on an island, one with a causeway that is twice daily covered by the tide. We know that the nearby town has a hotel called the Swan, with a proprietress by the name of Mrs Nicholson. Now, so far, so good. We have also learned through the good offices of Mr Jabez Wilson, that Tom George's assailants travelled via Liverpool Street Station. Now, if we add these relevant facts together, Doctor, we have the county, if not the exact town in that excellent county.'

A little deflated by his eloquence, I found myself agreeing with Holmes. I still had one question in my mind, however. 'Indeed,' I said, 'you have explained your deductions most clearly. But how did you come to the conclusion that Maldon was to be our final goal?'

'Well, now. You will agree that if Essex is our general destination, it follows that, as you say, somewhere has to be our final goal. My map of England showed me that the coastline of Essex has five possible islands to which I needed to turn my attention. I, therefore, required the good offices of another to help me there.'

'Quite so,' I said, 'but who . . .?'

'Ah, indeed. Who? That is the question I asked myself. The answer, I may say, was blindingly obvious.' He smiled. 'I therefore paid a visit on brother Mycroft and asked him to let me see the Admiralty Plans for the Essex coast.'

Holmes laughed. 'Well, he made a bit of a fuss and complained it was deucedly inconvenient. I suspect I was interrupting his luncheon plans. He did, however, accede to my request. Thus, with the information the map provided and the tide times listed in the accompanying information sheet, I was able to deduce pretty nearly exactly to which of the islands Tom George was referring. It had to be one of three: Mersea, near Colchester, or Northey and Osea near Maldon.'

He pulled another sheet of paper from his pocket. 'On my way from the Ministry, I stopped off at the British Library, where I was able to peruse the local Essex newspapers relevant to the areas in which I was interested.'

Holmes handed me the paper on which he had written a few lines.

'I believe this may also interest you. It is copied from the *Maldon Express.*'

It was my turn to laugh. 'My dear fellow,' I cried, 'this is excellent!'

The transcription read:

The Swan Hotel
Commercial and Posting House
Maldon, Essex
E.S. Nicholson, Proprietress

'So you see, Watson,' Holmes said, 'we have nearly all the evidence we need. All that remains now is to discover exactly which island is the correct one.'

In a little under an hour and ten minutes, the train slowly pulled into Witham. It was here we had to alight and change for Maldon. It was then we discovered that the train would not be along for nearly an hour. The porter who offered to assist us with our bags was most apologetic and suggested, if we were in a hurry, we would be best served by going into Witham and engaging a four-wheeler from the White Hart Hotel. Wishing to have the matter resolved as quickly as possible, Holmes and I accepted his advice and before long we were being driven at a brisk pace along the lanes of Essex.

For a short while the road ran close to the Maldon branch line, then it struck out to the west and past a large farmhouse, which the driver named as 'Oliver's Farm'. Then the road swung back to the east again and past several substantial properties, one of them, he informed us, was known as 'Stockhall'.

The road came in contact with the railway once more at Langford. We crossed over the line and headed down into the final part of our journey, through Heybridge; then crossing the railway for the final time, we found ourselves at last in Maldon.

'S'just down 'ere, sir,' said the driver in his warm East Anglian tones. 'Down Cromwell 'Ill, right into Silver Street an' the Swan's on yer right, opposite the church.'

The hotel façade proved to be of an early and substantial Georgian design. Holmes led the way and we were quickly confronted by the proprietress in person. He came immediately to the point. 'Good day, madam. My name is Sherlock Holmes and this is my friend and colleague, Dr Watson. I believe you are in the habit of taking in letters for a friend of ours, Tom George.'

The good lady smiled. 'Welcome, Mr Holmes, Dr Watson. Your fame has spread even to the wilds of the Blackwater Estuary. So you are friends of old Tom? From what I have recently seen, he needs all the friends he can get.'

'Really, Mrs Nicholson?' said Holmes, artlessly. 'Whatever do you mean?'

'Well, sir, last Wednesday it was. Two men were drinking in the lounge when Tom came in. He saw them and it seemed to me he tried to make sure they didn't see him. I don't blame him, mind. They weren't the sort of fellows I'd want to have too much to do with.' She moved behind the counter. 'A drink, gentlemen?'

'Thank you,' I said.

'Indeed,' agreed Holmes. 'Two glasses of your finest beer, if you please.'

The lady quickly produced two foaming glasses. Holmes took a deep draught. 'Excellent,' he exclaimed. 'Now, Mrs Nicholson. What exactly happened to Mr George?'

'Well, sir. I could see he weren't none too pleased to see 'em. Then I saw one of 'em take his arm and pull him aside, and there appeared to be a few heated words between 'em. Then Tom suddenly head-butts one of 'em and knocks him spinning into his mate. Then Tom's off like the wind down Silver Street towards the bridge. After pulling themselves together, the two of them collected themselves and rushed off after him.

'Then, I suddenly realized Tom's bicycle was still there. I wondered if I should take it in for safety's sake until Tom came back for it. But what d'you know? He's back again. He jumps on the machine and rides off like stink, just as the two show up. All I can hear is them shouting oaths after him.'

Mrs Nicholson laughed. 'Y'know, sir, I really had to smile. If only they had known where to find Tom, they could have gone out right after him. But I don't s'pose he left 'em his forwarding address. So anyway, they lost him. Well, they come back into the lounge and ordered a couple of drinks. They quickly drank up and left. Haven't seen 'em since. Likewise old Tom. Still I can't say I blame him for lying low for a bit. If I were him I'd not want to bump into them two rogues again.'

The lady briskly walked over to the table and chairs by the window and began to organize the cutlery.

Sherlock Holmes looked grimly at me. I cleared my

throat. 'Mrs Nicholson, I believe you should prepare yourself for some distressing news about Mr George. Mr Holmes and I believe him to have been the victim of a murderous assault.'

The lady sat down heavily on an adjacent chair. Her eyes became moist with emotion. 'You mean them men got to him after all, Dr Watson?'

'I am afraid so.'

'But how are you so certain? After all, you have only just arrived in Maldon.'

Holmes lay a comforting hand on the lady's shoulder. 'Unfortunately, we have prior knowledge in the shape of five phonograph cylinders, which have recently come into our possession.'

Mrs Nicholson wiped her eyes. 'The phonograph,' she said. 'I remember when he first got that machine. Old Walton McCarthy, the solicitor, sold it to Tom when he retired last December.' She smiled at the thought. 'It was probably the only item of value he ever owned in his life.'

Sherlock Holmes and I looked at each other, once more acutely aware of the value and burden of prior knowledge.

'Indeed,' said Holmes. 'Now, Mrs Nicholson, we need to locate Mr George, if only to make the final arrangements.'

Mrs Nicholson sighed and stood up. 'I shall be able to make the necessary disposals. This establishment supplies all that kind of thing.'

Holmes quickly finished his beer. 'Now, does the town have a senior policeman?'

The lady shook her head. 'Not for the present, Mr Holmes. The sergeant is away and we have a temporary man from Chelmsford, name of Brundle.' She looked at the longcase clock. 'About this time of day he's usually to be found in the courthouse on the London Road. If you like, I'll send the lad round to fetch him. In the meantime, I'm sure cook will make you some sandwiches and coffee.'

While the boy was gone, Mrs Nicholson joined Holmes and myself before a roaring fire in her private office and reminisced on the kindness and gentleness of Tom George. Full well she knew about his dark past, yet quite evidently she still held him in high regard. Fortunately, she also was keen to give Holmes and myself the relevant information, that he was a resident of Osea Island.

Almost twenty minutes passed before the sergeant was found. When eventually he arrived, rather red-faced and breathless, Sherlock Holmes soon acquainted him with the facts.

'Oh my, sir,' he said, clearly perturbed by the seriousness of our business. 'I'm not entirely sure if this is quite my line, murder an' that.'

Holmes stood up and, from the table, he collected his hat and coat. 'In your line or not, Sergeant, the matter has to be attended to without delay.'

Grumbling, the policeman followed Holmes and myself from the lounge of the hotel and into a waiting four-wheeler. Holmes goaded the horses into life and moments later we were heading for Osea Island and our appointment with the late Tom George.

Very soon we found ourselves once more in Heybridge. Holmes clearly knew the way, for he did not look to the left, nor to the right, but continued without reference to Sergeant Brundle or to a map. Through Heybridge we rattled. The smoke from the ironworks filling the air quite reminded me of Mr Charles Dickens's reference to the 'London Particulars' which were so common in town.

Then we were onto the Chigborough Road and very soon came in sight of the 'Old Windmill' at Barrowhill. Sergeant Brundle pointed out the two remaining sails. Now we could see over the Blackwater. In the middle distance, for the first time, our destination came into sight.

'There she is, sir,' cried the sergeant. 'Osea Island.'

A sign marked 'Jehu's Farm' came up on our left. Sherlock Holmes slowed the horses. To our right lay a rough track. Then, for the first time since our journey commenced, Holmes spoke. 'Our way is a little more uneven than I had anticipated,' he said, as he manoeuvred the vehicle through the gateway. 'Hold tight, Watson, Sergeant.'

Along the track we bounced and rattled, then we were at the water's edge. Before us lay a long snaking causeway. Osea Island with its rash of mature elms lay before us.

As the causeway had recently emerged from the tide, it was consequently both wet and slippery and it took all of Holmes's undoubted skill as a driver not to upset us into the muddy waters that lapped below our wheels.

Then at last we were on Osea. The roadway skirted the north of the island then turned into the tiny clutch of houses that nestled at its heart.

'Have you been to Osea before, Sergeant?' I asked.

'No, sir,' replied the policeman. 'I've only been seconded to this division for a few weeks and I've never had no need to come here.'

'Hm . . . that is a pity,' said Holmes. 'It would have made our task somewhat easier. However, I expect we shall find what we are seeking nevertheless.'

Holmes pulled up the four-wheeler, close by to the tiny

village store. As I jumped down, I could not help but notice the post office box and the legend it bore: 'The next collection will be subject to the tide.'

Nearby to the store, an elderly man, wearing a very old and battered billycock, was sitting on a settle, smoking a briar.

'Good day to you, sir,' cried Sherlock Holmes. 'Can you tell me where I might find Mr Tom George?'

The old man took his pipe out of his mouth and regarded us contemplatively. 'Indeed, sir,' he replied in a broad East Anglian accent, 'if you look down the road a-ways, you'll see Osea Cottage. That's his place. But I doubt if you'll find him. He seems to have gone away.'

'Oh dear, that is most awkward,' said Holmes, guilelessly. 'You see, my friends and I have come all the way from London today to see old Tom.'

'Ar, well, you can but try his house, I s'pose,' he said, jamming his pipe back into his mouth.

Holmes tipped his hat to the old man. 'Thank you for your assistance, sir. We shall take your advice with caution.'

Osea Cottage proved to be the first in a terrace of three, two-storeyed wooden properties. It also had a glass lean-to over the entrance.

I took Holmes by the arm. 'This could be unpleasant, old man,' I warned. 'If we are correct in our surmise, the late Mr George has lain dead in this cottage for the best part of three days, and if he was brutally attacked, we can expect considerable disorder.'

Holmes smiled his quick smile. 'My dear fellow . . .'

Sergeant Brundle said nothing. He merely looked uncomfortable.

'Very well, Watson,' said Holmes firmly, 'let us commence.'

Quite as expected, the door was firmly locked. The situation did not remain unresolved for long, however, as Holmes produced a leather pouch containing several solid-looking brass instruments with which he was swiftly able to pick the lock.

Sergeant Brundle gave a grunt. 'It's no wonder you are able to produce so many remarkable coups, Mr Holmes. We in the police force have to rely on more legitimate methods for our results.'

Holmes made no comment. He quickly replaced the pouch in its place of concealment and pushed open the door. Peering in, I could see little evidence of damage. Holmes made a sign for Brundle and myself to remain in the lean-to whilst he commenced to search the room.

After a few minutes, he bade us enter. He looked concerned. 'There is something wrong here, Watson.'

'What on earth do you mean, Holmes?' I said.

'Why, everything looks perfectly normal, sir,' remarked the sergeant.

'And that is precisely what is wrong.'

Holmes waved his hand in a gesture that resembled a conductor leading an orchestra. 'Ask yourself this, Watson. Would not a fierce struggle result in considerable damage? Yet there is nothing untoward to be observed.'

'What does it mean, Holmes?' I asked.

'It means we shall have to look elsewhere.'

At that moment, we were interrupted by a cry from the garden. It was Sergeant Brundle. 'Mr Holmes. Come quickly. Something is happening in the shed at the back!'

Holmes was through the door in a moment. Quickly, I pursued my companion. In the garden, Sergeant Brundle was standing before a large shed, peering through an almost obscured window.

'Over here, sir.'

Holmes took one quick look through the window. 'Watson!' he cried, 'I need your assistance. Quickly, man!'

Quite perplexed by this sudden turn of events, I followed Holmes around the shed.

'Help me break down the door.'

Together we placed our shoulders against the door and pushed. The lock was no match for our combined weight and the door burst open.

From within the darkened interior, there came a weak voice. 'Is that help? Or have you come back for me?'

'It is help, my poor fellow,' said Holmes gently.

'Thank God!'

'Let us have some light in here,' said Holmes, stepping across the floor and ripping down the old piece of sacking that obscured much of the window. The bright afternoon light streamed in and for the first time, I clearly saw the figure of a man lying spreadeagled on the floor. He was bound hand and foot to four metal stakes that had been driven into the earth. His clothing was filthy and his face was streaked with dirt.

'Who is this poor fellow?' I asked.

Holmes gazed at me in some surprise. 'Why, Doctor, do you not recognize Tom George?'

'Tom George? Good Lord!'

If Sherlock Holmes had announced the crack of doom, I could not have been more startled.

'But he is dead!'

Holmes laughed. '*Au contraire*. Eh, Tom? Now, Watson, no more foolishness. Help me to release Mr George, then we shall see what we can do to ameliorate his condition.'

Very much later the same evening, a well-fed, indeed re-plete party sat before a blazing log fire in Mrs Nicholson's sitting room. It was Tom George, however, who had the greatest reason to be satisfied. I had been very surprised when, upon examination, Tom proved to be in a remarkably good condition. Clearly, he was somewhat battered and bruised by his encounter with Porritt and Clark. He was both hungry and thirsty, but when all things were considered, he had escaped quite lightly. His captors, he informed me, had considered executing him on the spot, but upon reflection, they decided to stake him out and leave him to starve, an end, in their opinion, that was more fitting for a traitor.

The next morning we bade farewell to our companions. There was a small crowd waving us away when we left the Swan, bound for Maldon Station. At the station, we briefly stood before its imposing edifice admiring it, when a young man appeared. He was carrying a notebook and he wore an earnest expression. 'Mr Sherlock Holmes?'

'I am he.'

'Good day, sir. Good day, Dr Watson. My name is King. I am from the *Maldon Express* newspaper. I believe you were instrumental in the release and rescue of one of our citizens. May I ask you a few questions, sir?'

Holmes gazed languidly at the eager young man. 'If you so desire, Mr King. My train, however, is quite imminent. So I beg you to be brief in your questioning.'

The young man took out a pencil and waited with it poised over his notebook. 'Now, sir, I believe you have come down from Baker Street especially to clear up the case?'

'Indeed.'

'I suppose it was a most difficult affair which has brought you to the very edge of disaster before, as Dr Watson has often described in the *Strand Magazine*. You saved Mr George?'

Even the normally sanguine Sherlock Holmes was somewhat taken aback by this rush of eloquence. However, he smiled and briefly glanced in my direction. 'Not at all, Mr King. It was a case the local constabulary, in the shape of Sergeant Brundle, had virtually completed. My part was merely to add a few final touches. If there is anyone you should be addressing at this point, then it is the excellent Sergeant Brundle.'

The young reporter gave Holmes a disappointed look, snapped shut his notebook and began to edge away.

As Holmes and I watched the swiftly disappearing Mr King, there came a loud whistle from the direction of the station. We turned and made our way to the platform.

'You are a strange fellow, Holmes,' I remarked. 'Giving the credit to another, when it is entirely your own.'

Holmes laughed. 'My dear fellow, the train is about to depart. There was insufficient time for a long interview.' He looked mischievously at me. 'And besides, do you suppose I would give my story to a newspaper man when I have my Boswell standing before me? I think not, Watson.'

It was approaching lunchtime when our train rattled and smoked into Liverpool Street Station. As the day had become rather cold and rainy, we decided to make immediately for Marcini's and luncheon.

As the cab rattled along the city streets, something about the recent events was still troubling me. 'Holmes?'

'Yes, my dear fellow.'

'There are one or two points about this case which continue to elude me.'

'Indeed?'

'How could you tell from which station Tom's assailants had come, and why did they steal the phonograph?'

'Well now,' said Holmes. 'The answer to the second question will in some measure answer the first. The theft of the machine was born out of pure malice. Porritt and Clark had no idea what it was or what it could do, although they clearly realized it to be valuable, and they simply could not help themselves. They had robbed Tom of his wealth and in order to twist the knife in the wound, they stole the only item of value they could find. It is quite clear they had no use for it because they cleared it off their hands as soon as they could.

'Now I come to the matter of how I deduced that Porritt and Clark had come from Liverpool Street. You will recall Mr Jabez Wilson informing us that they were en route to a bank in Holborn? Now, Watson, a quick glance at any map of London will confirm that, if we are walking to Holborn from a station via Saxe Coburg Square, then the only possible deduction is that it is Liverpool Street from which we have come. The route from any other station would have taken us nowhere near to that most excellent square.'

I clapped my hands in applause. 'Of course,' I said. 'You are exactly right.'

'I will admit, Doctor, that good fortune decreed Mr Wilson's establishment should be on their route. We did, however, make the very most of that good fortune.'

'Do you suppose that Tom will ever see his money again?' I said.

Holmes was enigmatic in his reply. 'Perhaps, Doctor,

perhaps. Let us merely say that if the telegram you so diligently sent to Inspector Patterson has achieved the expected results, then he may.'

'That reminds me, Holmes: just who is the "friend" you expect Patterson to apprehend in Limehouse?'

'Why, Maury Attlee, of course.'

'Hmm,' I mused. 'I suspect there is considerably more to this than meets the eye.' I sighed. 'I do believe, however, we have encountered sufficient unto the day, and there is Marcini standing at his door.'